She

Watches

Me

Bury

Her

By
Alexander Engel-Hodgkinson

SHE WATCHES ME BURY HER

Copyright © 2018 by Alexander Engel-Hodgkinson

ISBN 978-1-989331-01-9

Art by Alexander Engel-Hodgkinson

Published by
Dark Brothers Incorporated

Author's Comment

My best horror concepts seem to revolve around domestic disputes or a family in crisis. Hmmm. After the reception I received for *I Keep My True Love in the Basement* and its */REMIX* version (overall warm, though some saw the domestic angle as sexist and distasteful), I've been a bit hesitant to explore that side of horror again. But here I am. Exploring it. Because sometimes, you can't keep good inspiration down, no matter what some people tell you.

Funny thing is, the house the Morgans live in is actually inspired by my grandmother's (on my mother's side) house. I liked the house and the location. I did not like its owner. At all.

SHE WATCHES ME BURY HER

Part One: Friday, October 20th, 2000

I'm in a dark room filled with neon blue, populated by black shadows with minds of their own. The walls are bare; there are no windows or even doors. The ceiling, I think, is stucco, but the stucco seems to move if you stare at it long enough. I can't decide what the floor looks like, even when I look at it. I don't know where the blue light comes from. It's like being underwater without the water.

I turn around and I see two black holes in the wall, real empty and wide, as if the wall has opened its eyes to stare at me. I hear a woman's airy voice overlapped and distorted by the deep voice of a man with a smoker's rasp: "Enter me." Then a mouth opens between the eyes, big enough for me to walk through, and for some reason I do that even though I don't want to because its mouth is just as black and empty as its eyes.

So I walk inside its mouth into another room. Pitch black. The mouth and eyes close behind me, trapping me in this new darkness. I feel like the darkness is touching me with a multitude of hands, groping me, tickling me, scratching me, digging into my skin until I say "Stop" a few times, and eventually they do.

Red burning light fills the other side of this room, revealing to me a high-ceilinged cavern with walls that are too far to see. A black figure stands in front of me. It would look human if it didn't look like it'd been stretched tall and thin; it resembled a smear on a wall, but I knew it wasn't a smear on a surface because it started pacing back and forth with these long, thin legs, wobbling forward and backward, forward and backward.

It stops eventually. A pair of eyes appears on its face and stares at me. Then the eyes float off the face and rise high above the body, still fixed on me, probing me.

Somebody says, "Ever see a living thing cut to pieces?"

I shake my head.

"Do you want to?"

The stretched figure loses a hand. It squeaks. It loses a leg and keels over, screaming. Its body splits in half. A gurgled, desperate cry for help bubbles up from its throat as more pieces of it fall off and slither away.

Someone whispers, "Wake up."

My name is Cameron Morgan, and I hate my life. I'm a dedicated father of three beautiful children. Unfortunately, I'm also married to a witch, stuck in a house in the woods with no way out—no way that makes sense.

I wake up at 5:30 AM every morning to take the padlocks off the kids' bedroom doors before fixing the door to my own shared bedroom, as normally it's on the floor or hanging by a single hinge by the time I'm up. My wife is still sound asleep on her side of the bed, and will sleep through the entire twenty minutes it normally takes to repair the door.

Around 5:50 AM, I take a shower, brush my teeth, and enjoy my freedom while I can—all while listening to the early morning news on the radio.

It's 6:30 AM. Time for breakfast. Kids wake up to a warm bowl of oatmeal every Monday, Wednesday, and Friday; and a cool bowl of cereal every Tuesday and Thursday. On the weekends, my wife or I make them something special, like French toast or omelettes. Routine is good.

7:00 AM. Time to get ready for school. The kids do their hygiene, get dressed, pack their bags, and by the time they're finished with all of that, I'm done making their lunches.

7:45 AM. Kids traverse silently down the driveway and disappear behind the slope and board the bus without a word. Now I'm alone in the house.

Alone… with *her*. Only a few more hours until she wakes up. I try to remember what happened last night. It's different every time. So many different things, all my memories colliding, distorting as they merge together. Makes it hard to remember what happened at which time; which thing occurred, what I used, what sparked it.

I walk through the house. Mary's room is clean and full of pink and overcrowded with stuffed animals. Todd and Michael's room is as blue this morning as it was last night. Computer on the desk, shelf stocked with books, the bunk bed in the corner, the wall of sliding mirrors for the closet on the other side, the late-nineties CRT TV with the built-in VCR and attached gaming console…

looks fine, although the door has a few more scratches than it did the night before. Something's sticking out of it—a splinter? No. I peer closer. A fingernail. I pluck it out and move on.

I already know the bathroom is okay. Kitchen's fine. Dining room's fine. I pass through the kitchen to get into the living room and it's exactly the way I left it, too. I enter the dining room; turn left to the small area leading to the rear balcony and swimming pool—all of which are fine. Swimming pool still has the cover on, and it's still blue. Good. Having to clean out the pool always sucked. Luckily I spared myself that agony last night.

I turn away from the screen door leading to the balcony toward another door, this one solid oak. I unlock it and step into the garage. My car, a cobalt blue 1972 Dodge Charger, sits under the garage's fluorescent light tubes. There's a small red patch beside it, dried into the concrete. That's gonna take some scrubbing. I search around the car and nothing else is out of the ordinary. I step out into the driveway and look up at the cedars, white birch, and maple trees that dwarf the house in comparison, surrounding us, boxing us in. Their leaves turned yellow and orange, dictated by the season to eventually fall out of their place in the canopy and flutter to the earth and accumulate over time until they're all the human eye can see.

I follow the flagstone path around the side of the house into the back. Some of the flagstones have red on them. Not much. Shouldn't take more than a few hours. For the next hour, I scrub the flagstones clean with dish soap and stain remover, and for the following two hours, I use a sponge to scrape tirelessly at the dark stain in the garage until it's nothing but a heavily faded, barely noticeable memory. I dump the bucket in the grass, throw away my rubber gloves, and return to the end of the flagstone path in the backyard. It's all dirt and mud now, the once picture perfect grass long since eviscerated by shovels. A hole in the twisted mounds gapes at me.

The body I put in the ground last night has been unearthed.

It's 10:54 AM now. She'll be up in an hour or so. I pop the tab off a can of beer and sit in front of the TV, watching whatever I can before she wakes up. There isn't much on TV. Never can find anything good to watch late in a weekday morning. Nothing but reality TV and staged talk shows. The talk shows are slightly more interesting. I get to see would-be parents try to prove to one another that they're actually related to their children. "You *are* the father!" the talk show host will say, or "You are *not* the father!" Either way, the crowd cheers on, and someone on the stage collapses in disbelief, usually in tears.

I look up, for no real reason at all, at the corner above my head. I see a fly entangled in a spider's web, wriggling in its threads, trying to get free. Its struggles only exacerbate its situation. The spider, a black, ugly, monstrous little thing, crawls toward it...

12:13 PM. Something in my peripherals makes my head snap to the left. There she is. Maureen, my wife, tall and thin, her messy black hair curling and drooping over her tired face and brushing the tops of her shoulders. Dressed in one of my shirts that stops at her thighs and probably nothing else. "Morning," she mutters quietly.

I set my beer on a coaster on the coffee table. "Morning." It begins.

"Did you eat?" she asks.

I sweep my hand in the direction of my beer.

"Oh," she says, "that's no good."

I shrug. Watching her like a domestic cat watches a new dog the family just brought home.

"I'll make something." She leaves. I listen to her drag her feet across the living room's pinewood floor and then the kitchen's linoleum floor. She calls out, "Cameron."

"What?"

"The dishes aren't done."

I sigh and get up off the couch. "Coming." I enter the kitchen and start filling the sink with hot soapy water. I start scrubbing the plates from yesterday while she mutters to herself. I only catch a few words, but I know she's quietly ranting to herself about how much she regrets marrying me while she busies herself with making our breakfast. "What're you making?"

"What's it matter? You're gonna eat it anyway."

Passive-aggressive attitude's back in spades. I shrug with indifference and exhale slowly, trying my best to ignore her. Focus on the dishes. I rinse a freshly cleaned plate under the tap and set it sideways on the rack. "Whatever."

"What's with the sighing?" Here we go. "Think you have it rough? Poor Cameron. You have a roof over your head, a wife who loves you for reasons she can't even begin to explain or understand by herself; hell, you barely have to cook anything except oatmeal for the kids three days a week. Yeah. Poor Cameron. You have it *so* hard." She slams a skillet on the stovetop with a loud *crash*, startling me. "Earth to Cameron!"

"What the fuck do you *want*?" I snap.

She stabs a slender forefinger at me, green eyes blazing bitterly. "Watch it," she says, her pitch low and threatening.

I stare back, defiant. We hold, unblinking, one refusing to back down to the other. Eventually, I fold. Not because she has anything on me, but because I figure the dishes are more important than getting petty satisfaction from coming out on top in a squabbling session with her. I let her have her victory.

She takes it and continues preparing breakfast. Doesn't take me long to notice she's making French toast and eggs. Again.

12:57 PM. Sunny side up. Two golden yolks glisten on both sides of my stacked French toast slices. I thank her for the meal as she sits down at the opposite end of the table with her own plate. She grunts, and that's the only acknowledgement she's willing to give me.

Her eggs are scrambled.

We eat our meal in silence. When we finish, we put our dishes in the sink.

"You going to do them now?" she asks me. "Or are you gonna wait for them to pile up?"

"I'll do them tonight."

She fixes me with a hard look.

"I promise," I add.

1:43 PM. Maureen's out back on the porch, doing something that isn't bothering me. I return to the TV, on those reality shows, on who *is* the father, who *is not* the father. I glance back up at the spider's web above me. The spider's resting in the darkest corner of its web. Its latest catch is cocooned in silk near the center. It wiggles helplessly in its tiny prison.

2:18 PM. Maureen sits down in her favourite armchair by the fireplace. She squints at the TV. "Can't you ever watch anything worth seeing?"

"Like what? It's early afternoon on a weekday."

"But it's Friday."

"So what?"

"They usually have better shows on."

"Not this early."

"They used to."

"Well, they don't *now*."

"I miss when TV used to be fun."

I don't reply.

"Wouldn't you agree?"

"About what?"

"TV used to be fun."

"Used to be? What do you mean, 'used to be'?"

"When we were younger, I mean."

"I didn't *have* a TV when I was younger. I didn't have a TV until I married you. I played outside. I had friends. There were better things to do than watch TV."

I don't have to look at her to know that she's pursing her lips in a bitter scowl like she always does when I talk to her.

"Let's do that, then."

"Do what?"

"Let's have some fun. Let's go out. Do something."

"Like what?"

"*Anything*, if it means getting out of this house."

"We have a pool."

"In the fall? Come on. Nobody goes swimming in the fall."

"Exactly," I reply, pretending that I've answered her question. "That's why I bought us a pool, Maureen. Go for a swim, if you wanna do something fun. I bought you a pool so you could have fun outside, in the sun. I *bought* it, out of my own pocket, because you wanted it. Go play in the pool, Maureen. Go play in the pool, and let me watch my fucking television."

For a while, she doesn't make a sound. I ignore her stare and I keep my eyes on the TV screen. If I look at her, she wins and she knows it. I don't let her win.

She springs from her chair and leaves in a huff, her feet heavy on the pinewood floor.

I lean back and watch my TV. "You *are* the father!" it declares.

3:19 PM. I step out on the porch by the pool for a stretch, and to check up on her. She's lounging on a lawn chair reading a romance novel out on the patio. The dog house sits under the dining room window behind her. The chain has been coiled around in the dirt for so long that parts of it have been swallowed up by the earth. The collar, frayed and faded, sits near the edge of the patio. She hasn't asked about him, yet. Maybe she won't today. We once managed to go a whole week without her asking about Buster. It's better when she doesn't.

I can't stop myself from looking beyond the porch at the earth she disturbed last night.

3:55 PM. The kids come home. The rollercoaster's about to begin. They resign to their rooms to do their homework or play their games. I'm not too worried if it's something that doesn't involve their mother. Saves me the stress of worrying about them.

Maureen's still reading on the patio. She doesn't see me looking at her through the slats I nailed over the dining room's picture window. Maybe she just knows these things. I can't always tell with her.

5:43 PM. Dinnertime. Maureen made us roast beef and scalloped potatoes with steamed carrots and string beans on the side. We sit around the table and eat. Only the sounds of silverware scraping on our plates, and the occasional cough, are heard.

At first.

"There are lots of dishes to be done now," Maureen said as she sliced her scalloped potatoes into little pieces. "You let them pile up."

I sigh. "Maureen, we've been over this a hundred thousand times…"

"Oh, I'm sorry," Maureen replies sarcastically, glaring at me from across the table. The kids keep eating with their heads low on either side of the table between us. "Am I starting to annoy you? You keep *doing* it a hundred thousand times, so I have to keep bringing it up! Maybe if you stopped procrastinating, you wouldn't be hearing about it anymore. You could do that instead of numbing yourself in front of the TV."

I try to warn her, "Maureen—"

"You think I *enjoy* talking to you about this? You know how I just *hate* having to repeat myself!"

"SHUT UP!" Startled screeches from the kids' silverware

when they jump. Then everything is silent. The knife has sliced a thin layer through the tension. The noise in the dining room reduced to a silent flat line. I glance at each of the three little sets of eyes staring at me in turn. The children are terrified. I hate fighting in front of them. Maureen thinks it gives her an edge, though she would never admit it.

Now she's pretending to be hurt by my outburst, staring right through me with empty eyes.

I peer over my plate, taking deep breaths, trying to suppress my rage as much as I can. I mutter, "Just shut the fuck up."

Her eyes dart to the knife in my hand, and then drop to her plate. She doesn't say another word.

6:29 PM. Family time. We all sit down in front of the TV in time for the nightly movie—the original *Don't Be Afraid of the Dark*. Whenever something even remotely creepy occurs onscreen, I instinctively look at the kids to see how they're handling it. Of course, they're fine. Stone-faced, even. They live with much worse, day by day. A TV movie from the seventies is a cakewalk.

"Anyone want hot chocolate?" I ask the kids.

Maureen pretends I included her: "Yes."

I hide my scowl and ask our youngest daughter of four years: "Mary?"

"Yes, please," she chirps.

"Todd?"

Our oldest son, turning ten next summer, answers, "Sure, dad."

Six-year-old Michael says, "I want one, too. With extra marshmallows."

I nod and head into the kitchen to fill the kettle with water. Maureen follows me, circles the table behind me. Our children are alone in the living room, and she keeps her voice low so they can't hear what we're about to discuss. "When are you going to do those?" I know she's addressing the pile of dishes in the sink.

"Later."

"You said that earlier."

"I meant it earlier."

"What's that mean? You don't mean to do them now?"

"I'll do them later."

"You said that already."

"Look, I'll do them, just get off my back."

"*When* will you do them?"

I'm simmering. "After."

"After *what*, Cameron?" She spits my name like it's the most disgusting thing she's ever had in her mouth. "You always say you're gonna do it, then when I wake up it's *still* not done."

The kettle begins to steam.

I keep my voice low. I don't turn around. "I'll do them tonight."

"When?"

"*Tonight*, Maureen. Promise. Now get off my back."

"That's what you said last night. That's what you said this morning, too!"

"Goddamn it, Maureen, I'll *do* them."

"Bullshit, you will! More empty promises. 'I promise to do this, I promise to do that.'"

Kettle's pitch rises.

I'm shaking.

"'I promise, promise, promise!' Yeah, you're full of shit. Nothing but bullshit! You hear me, Cameron? *Bullshit*! Empty, unfulfilling bullshit! Just like you, and this house, and this fucking marriage—"

The kettle squeals around me and ruptures when it collides with her face. Boiling water splashes the walls and the countertop. I hit her again. Water scalds my arm and the furious wrinkles on my face as I follow her to the floor and hit her again and again and again until more than just water splashes on the walls and the floor. I'm seeing red and lots of grey; grey from the bursts of steam rising in my face and stinging my eyes. I keep lifting the kettle off her face and then I bring it back down again and I bring it up and down, up and down, thunk, thunk, *thunk*...

And when I finally stop I realize the kids are standing at the edge of the living room the whole time, watching silently as I kill their mother again.

"Go back to the TV," I tell them. "Go on."

They hesitate.

My voice is sterner, more urgent: "*Go*."

They file back into the living room where I can't see them. Their shadows dance on the wall, flickering with the TV's glow, shifting colours, distorted on the glass doors of the bookshelf.

*

7:42 PM. Gave myself lots of time tonight. I take Maureen's ankles and drag her down the front ramp that leads to the driveway, then across the drive around to the far side of the house, following a different pathway this time, along the front garden. I pass a stone birdbath that'd been smashed on a different occasion, which I never bothered to clean up. I can't stop my eyes from drifting up to her face, which has been scalded and misshapen on the left side. Her cheekbone is shattered with a piece of it sticking up just under her swollen eye, penetrating the skin and oozing blood onto her mouth, which partly hangs open. The moonlight reflecting off her white teeth reveals a few gaps that weren't there before. As I pass the kids' bedroom windows, boarded up on the outside and sealed shut with nails on the inside—the boards are all covered in scratches and red streaks—I notice her good eye is bulging wide in angry disbelief at me. Finally, we're on the grass and passing the water pump toward the work shed that sits crookedly on cinderblocks at the edge of the forest. An owl hoots above me. The crickets cheer when they see Maureen's body being pulled through the soft grass.

When I reach the shed, I unlock the door and throw it open. It bangs loudly against the wall. I switch on the low-hanging light bulb, drowning the shack's cramped interior in deep red as a grim reminder of another night I had to drag her out here. No... taking her head off didn't stop her, but it *did* slow her down. It *did* buy me time.

I look back down the two steps at her face. Her petrified eye stares back at me. My neck tingles. A thousand insects slither and crawl up my spine. Maybe if I stare at her long enough she'll leap up and grab me and tear me to shreds.

Can't let my imagine run wild like that. Not right now.

I hold my breath, mustering up the courage to lift her off the ground and carry her into the shed. I lay her down on the work bench and chain her down. I lean outside; scan what I can see of the front yard and then the backyard, especially the porch. The two bedroom windows on the side of the house are dark and empty. They watch indifferently. The three basement windows below them form a straight, black Jack-o'-Lantern mouth for the two square eyes above them. They're also boarded up, and the boards here are scratched, too, but the damage on these covers doesn't compare to the kids' rooms. The boards are necessary for every window. The house can't see what I'm doing.

SHE WATCHES ME BURY HER

Snap out of it, Cameron. The house doesn't give a shit.

I yank the door shut and drop the clasp securely. It's just me and her in this dark red room, with a wooden shelf stocked full of power tools and a couple of plastic recycling bins tucked under the work bench.

She starts suddenly, and gurgles, chokes on something. My heart jumps and I leap back against the shelf, watching her wriggle in her restraints, spitting blood and finally, a tooth. Her eye spins wildly around as she tries to get her bearings. Her hair wet and sticky with blood leaking out of the gash the kettle opened across the side of her cranium curls over her face in messy clumps and strands. She looks at me, confused, terrified, *betrayed.* "Cameron…?"

"Stop."

"Cameron, wuh…?"

I whirl around and grab the chainsaw.

Her eye goes wide. Her struggling intensifies, becomes more violent. "Cameron! Cameron, no! Cameron!"

"Shut up, witch. Shut up. Shut up." I wrestle the cord, trying to get the damn thing to start. It sputters again and again. "Shut up. Shut up. Shut up."

"Cameron!"

"You made me do this. You made me do this. This is your fault. This is *your* fault, you evil little bitch!"

"Stop! Stop. Cameron, please, s-stop. You don't need to—"

The chainsaw roars to life. It's deafening within the tight confines of the shack. I talk over the motor's stuttering growls. "Yes, I do."

"Cameron, stop! Think, think of the kids. Think of them. What they'd be like… without their mother. Please don't kill me. Please, Cameron, please, please, please."

"Shut up. Don't you dare use my kids. Don't you fucking dare."

She fixes me with that look again. Her one good eye quivers in its socket, her pupils shrinking as the white of her eye dims somewhat. "You never let me tuck them into bed."

"I can't."

"You can't keep me away from my children."

I raise the chainsaw for her to see. Her eye follows the blade as it hovers above her stomach. "They're not *your* children anymore." I steel myself. This is it.

Somebody says, "Ever see a living thing cut to pieces?"

The chainsaw descends like a guillotine and bites into her stomach, making her jolt. It sinks down inside her, disappearing in the folds of her flesh. The chainsaw's teeth spray her blood all over me and give the walls and ceiling a fresh coat of red. The lightbulb swings wildly above me, throwing the shadows into a chaotic dance across the walls.

Somewhere in her throat, she finds an ear-splitting scream to unleash on my ears, and I scream right back, blinded by the violent arterial spray shooting up from her middle and battering my front, pouring onto my face like a torrential rain, drenching me. I scream until it floods my mouth and I swallow some of it and spit the rest. It's bitter and warm on my tongue and it just won't stop—

I pull the chainsaw out of the black, gnarly gorge I just cut into her and wipe my face on my wet sleeve. A lot of good *that* does. Still dripping from the tip of my nose to the bottom of my chin. Still blind with her blood coursing down my face. The ceiling drips. *Pitter-patter-pitter-patter-pitter-patter.* I wipe the back of my hand across my eyes and forehead and look at the gruesome sight of her.

She's twitching, head rotating back and forth, fingers curling rigid and then relaxing and then curling again, her nails scraping against the work bench. But her eye never leaves me. Not for one second does it stray...

I'll make it stray, and her neck is the next thing I saw through, turning my face away so that the side of my head takes the worst of the inevitable spray. Once I have her head detached, I scrape it over the side of the bench into a recycling bin below. It lands with a dull *thud*.

No time to dwell. I get to work on the rest of her.

8:13 PM. I manage to fit all of her in one recycling bin and I carry it around the pool and dump her body parts into the hole. I leave her pieces scattered in the five-foot pit for only a minute to get the spade, which is stored under the porch, and I return and immediately start shoveling dirt back into the hole. Her head is propped up on a rock and cradled by her left arm, facing up. Even in death, her eye never leaves me. It never strays. I throw dirt on it. Her head is the first thing I bury. The rest of her is eventually covered up—

Something's wrong. I straighten my back and immediately my

eyes are drawn to the blackness of the forest. There isn't a sound in there. No wind rustling through the leaves. No crickets. Is there something in there? "Is there anybody out there?"

Of course, no one answers.

But I know that there's *someone* out there, someone who *could* answer, who *won't*. Someone or some*thing*.

I can't stop. I have to bury her. I still have another foot to go, and as I fill in the hole I pray harder than I did the night before. Please, God, *please*, let the bitch *stay dead this time*.

9:01 PM. The first thing I do when I go back inside the house (after locking the door and checking the locks on the garage door and the shutters) is check on the kids. They're safely gathered on the couch in front of the TV. My strong little warriors. They don't know how proud I am. If only they understood.

I don't want them to see me as I am now; caked in dark layers of their mother's drying blood and dirt, so I go to the bathroom—locking the front door on my way—and drop my clothes into a garbage bag and tie the knot. I shower and scrub myself down and wash all the gore and dirt and muddy clumps down the drain as quickly as I can. I get out and get dressed in casual clothes and I return to the living room. Just leaving them out here is a gamble, even if it *is* a while yet before she wakes up. "Okay, kids... bedtime."

Todd and Michael get up and leave the room to brush their teeth.

Little Mary sleeps peacefully on the arm of the couch, dreaming of a better world. I gather her up in my arms and she clings to me in her sleep, rests her face against my chest as I carry her down the corridor to her bed, where I tuck her in, give her forehead a kiss, and turn on her nightlight. Then I leave, shut her door, and snap the padlock into place.

By this point, the boys are done getting ready. They're in their pajamas and lying in their designated levels on the bunk with the light already off. I lean into the room. "Good night, boys."

No reply.

"I love you."

Nothing. I understand, but it saddens me all the same. They probably think *I'm* the evil one. They probably hate me. Maybe they're afraid of me, too.

Of course they are. Of course they're afraid. They have every right to be scared. I'm scared, too.

I shut their door. The padlock clicks as I force the shackle into the body.

10:50 PM. With the kids locked safely in their rooms, I'm busy running a security check on the house. All the windows are still boarded and secure. The doors are locked and bolted. The basement door is… open. I don't remember leaving it open like that. I peer down the stairwell, which curves to the left. It's a fully liveable basement, fully furbished.

I descend the stairs and switch on every light as I check all the rooms before I pass the back of the staircase on my way to the other end of the basement. The bar, the couch and the TV in the lounge across from the bar; the bathroom and the laundry room accessible through a small entryway beside the TV—all clear. By the time my search for anything out of the ordinary is complete, every lamp and light bulb is on. The place is musty and clearly a product of the seventies. I didn't replace any of the furnishings; the green plaid fold out couch flanked by two table lamps with stained glass shades, the golden swag lamp hanging by the bar, the half partition walls made of elegantly carved oak lined with a wide assortment of old trinkets and toys. The orange shag carpet with brown diamond patterns was ugly, but I wasn't about to uproot the damn thing because of that. I didn't even take down the beaded curtains that were put up over every doorway down here. All left behind from the house's first owners, the Thorns, as seen in the wood-carved sign hanging above the bar: THORN FAMILY PUB.

For a second, I almost forgot why I was down here. I double-check all the rooms before I shut all the lights off and run back upstairs, closing the door behind me.

For the next little while, I turn on the radio and listen to a classic rock station while I busy myself with mopping Maureen's blood off the kitchen floor. And then, just to spite the bitch, I wash the dishes.

By the time I'm finished, the clock is approaching midnight. Still have time to write an update in my journal. My heart thumps heavily in my ears. It's almost time. It's almost time. It's almost…

Part Two: Witching Hour, Saturday, October 21st, 2000

12:15 AM. They call it the witching hour in folklore. Some say it's from three to four. Others say it's from midnight to two. For me... the witching hour starts at midnight and ends at six.

Five hours, forty-five minutes to go. May as well get comfortable, but I never can. This is the worst part. The part where I can't stop my hands from trembling and I can't sit still or lie comfortably in my bed because I know the bitch will be trying to find a new way to get in like she does every night.

At 12:30, I can't hear anything except for the radio.

At 12:45, I hear the wind howling outside. It's sudden, and the first sign of a storm approaching. God, you don't know the half of it. But she hasn't come out yet. She hasn't taken this long before. My method worked. It bought me more time. How much time, I'm not entirely sure yet, but it bought me something and so far that's good enough for me.

It's almost 1 AM and the howling turns to wailing, and I know that the wailing isn't the wind, it's *her*. She's back and she's angry and frantic and manic and emotional because the children are inside here with me and she's out there with her shitty personality. The wails drone on and on and on, rising and falling as she circles the house. It's a desperate cry for help, like an injured animal suffering a fate worse than death. Shrill, psychotic moans echo through the house. A banshee's cries.

Oh, kids... I hope you're asleep.

I sit in the living room with the lights off and I don't dare turn them on and I sure as hell keep away from the windows. Boarded or not boarded, sometimes I wonder what difference they would make if Maureen were stronger than she was.

And on that thought, I catch her shadow streaking through the slants of the living room window as she quickly ascends the ramp without making a sound. Then the screen door opens and the main door rattles as she fights the lock. She twists the knob back and forth and kicks the screen door and—I think this time she ripped it right out of its hinges! I hear the screen smacking the porch banister as it crashes into the garden.

"CAMERON!" she shrieks, pounding her fists on the last door. "OPEN THIS DOOR! LET ME IN! LET ME *IIIIIIIIINNN*!"

I listen to her in the dark, eyeing the wall beside the TV that the front door hides behind. Pound that door all you want. You're never getting in. I would sooner die than let you in here.

I repeat my vows in my head over and over again, trying to flood out her screaming with my thoughts. I will not let you in. I will not let you in. I will not let you—

Something crashes in the back. I hear it between Maureen's thunderclaps against the front door. What the hell made that noise? I bolt upright and use the shadows to keep from knocking anything over, making my way into the dining room. I look at the door leading to the small pool room. Nothing there.

Another crash. The deck's screen door bounces out of its frame and then swings back into place. Something's out there with her and it also wants to get in. But what else could be out there that would share her motive? I go to the windows and peek through the slats. There's the patio, and the pool beside it remains undisturbed. I can only see so much of the deck. I can't see what's out there from here, so I enter the pool room just as the outer door receives another loud beating that makes the screen door wobble forward. There's a little window beside the door that no one could fit through, and no one could conceivably reach in and unlock the door, as the two are a convenient distance away from each other. I never bothered to board this one up, and right now, I didn't dare get close to it to see who— or *what*—is out there. A hand could still break through it, after all.

The screen door clicks shut. The chest freezer drones behind me. Outside, the wailing seems distant. The pounding at the front door continues to rumble through the house like a rapid heartbeat.

Then, a sudden cry from just outside preludes a sharp kick at the door in front of me. It shudders, throwing the screen door out of its frame again. It springs back into place.

What the fuck is going on? I can't move. I jump at the initial impact, and that's the end of my movement for a short time while I stand there dreading the next impact.

A black shape moves swiftly across the window toward the patio. I rush to follow it into the dining room, and I peek through the slats of the picture window to see Maureen *floating* off the deck with without any legs to ground her with. Nothing below her midriff

SHE WATCHES ME BURY HER

exists but sinewy strands trailing off the bottom of her torso. Her arms are extended outward, fingers stretched longer than I've ever seen them before. They look like bloody phalanges torn out of a dragon's wings!

Jesus Christ, *no legs*! And where are her eyes? She doesn't have any eyes...

I snap out of my shock when I realize that the pounding at both doors hasn't stopped. I know for sure that Maureen is on the front porch, but she's *also* hovering above the patio in the backyard? Does that mean there are *two* Maureens now? *Two* copies of my wife?!

And what about the one on the porch? *Who* is trying to get into the pool room? A *third* copy?

Jesus Christ.

I draw away from the window. My head's swimming in my own confusion. What the fuck is going on? This never happened before. All those times I've killed Maureen, she never multiplied. After all these years I spent killing her again and again and again, she's never come back in twos or threes or fours.

Why now? Why is *now* so different?

She shatters my thoughts with the lawn chair when it smashes against the picture window. This floating half-Maureen is trying to break in the easy way. But it's *not* the easy way, because only a week after all of this first began, I still had money, and the sense to replace almost all the windows with somewhat crude-but-effective ballistic glass custom-made by a friend of mine working in a glass and mirror shop near Lake Ontario. Cost me a goddamned fortune, too.

She can bang away at that glass till her heart's content. She won't be breaking through anytime soon. She seems to know that, too, because now half-Maureen is screaming at the top of her lungs.

"What's that, Maureen?" I ask her. "You feeling a little under the weather?" I laugh. Sometimes all you can do is laugh. She keeps hitting the glass and I keep laughing. The lawn chair bends against the glass, then snaps somewhere in the middle, folding uselessly when she smashes it across the window again. Nothing but fabric holding it together now. My laughter explodes from within; it's a wheezing, grating, psychotic laugh that doesn't stop.

With a nails-on-the-chalkboard screech she flings the lawn chair over Buster's old house and makes a show of scuttling across the air as if it were solid ground, disappearing from my sight toward the shed. "What seems to be the trouble, Maureen?" I'm hooting and tittering, feeling my head tighten as my blood pressure builds from all the laughter. Tears start welling up in the corners of my eyes. She's still fighting the front door and the back door to the deck. Another racket momentarily stops me. A rattling, metallic staccato echoing from… *the garage*, that's it. Now she's struggling with *three* different entrances. I can feel my laughter bubbling up in my chest again.

Then I stop, because something else sounds out, something that grips me and jerks me out of my mirthful state.

It was brief—if one of Maureen's fists had struck any of the doors at the same time, it would have gone unheard. But they didn't, and I *did*. The sound, it…

"No…"

…It came from the basement. A sharp tinkling sound. My feet jettison me into the kitchen, legs feeling like rubbery as I follow the counter to the thirteen-piece knife block set next to the microwave. All of the knives are there except one: the cleaver. It's been that way for a long time, and I expected her to retaliate with it, but she never did.

I draw a chef's knife from its sheath, and then I tiptoe-dash past the fridge into the small foyer. I look at the front door and watch it tremble from Maureen's relentless hammering. The small chandelier hanging over it swings and rotates dangerously, threatening to plummet into the rug. I look to my left down the narrow corridor. It's dark and empty. All the doors are shut. Just to be safe, I tread lightly down the hall and check the locks on the children's doors. Still secure. Good.

Now, the basement. What made that noise? Could it have something to do with Maureen? I would have doubted it at first, but now that I know that she can multiply herself, I don't doubt it anymore. Either she's down there, or the rats have gotten bigger and clumsier. My money's on the former.

With the racket Maureen's making, there's no need to play it quiet. I throw the door open, switch on the light and descend the stairs with the knife raised for a fight. The house continues to shudder as I check each of the rooms thoroughly; under the beds, in the closets, all of the cupboards and drawers. When I'm done with them, I switch on another light on my way to the bar and the lounge slightly more relaxed. I don't see anything, but I *know* something fell in here, and *broke*. Now what was it?

I scan the carpet for anything out of the ordinary, roaming around the couch as I do so, and leaning into the laundry room when I pass the entrance. Nothing shows up until I start heading back and notice that the trinkets on the partition ledge have been disturbed. A little china teapot rests in pieces at the partition's base. But *what* disturbed it?

Something scrapes behind the bar and I whirl to face it, heart leaping into overdrive again. She's behind the bar. No. Maybe I'm just getting ahead of myself here. I *have* to be. I creep round the bar, trying to drown out the banging doors as I focus solely on the space behind the bar. She can't be there she can't be there she—

I jump around the corner and look down.

I catch a quick glimpse of a rat's mottled black fur as the fat, ugly little thing scuttles into a hole in the corner beneath the cupboard. Just a rat. Problematic, but not a priority. All this fear and excitement over a stupid rat.

2:11 AM. The banging has ceased. The Maureens outside are crying now. Occasionally I hear one of them claw at the windows or make another brief, furious attempt to break down the doors. She has passed her peak. Now she's weakening and breaking down emotionally.

I nurse a cold beer at the end of the dining room table, positioned so that I can comfortably glance through the slats between the wooden panels into the backyard whenever I spot movement. A dozen or so Maureens are roaming around the house and they all want in. They want the children. My children. She can't have them. she can *never* have them.

"I'm sorry, Buster."

My head swivels toward the picture window. Remorse? From *her*? I have to see this so I get out of my chair with my beer still in my hand and I stand in front of the picture window and look out to see Maureen curled in front of the dog house sobbing in her hands. Most of her flesh has returned, with a few dark red patches still prominent in some areas, mostly her joints. She's gripping Buster's collar with swollen pink fingers. "I'm sorry, boy. I'm so sorry. I couldn't help it."

A painful fire starts to burn in the emptiness that has long hollowed my body, as it always does when the past rears its ugly head to dig up things I would rather keep buried. Like Buster. Like Maureen. I don't know why I don't just clear it all away. Discard the collar. Tear down the dog house. Roll up the chain, or use it to keep Maureen locked underground longer.

She stops crying and looks up at me. Eyes wide and full of stark white, bulging with fear, anger, hatred, sadness. It's a piercing look. A frenzied, terrifying look. Staring back at her only seemed to make ice-cold fingers creep up my spine and tickle the hairs on my neck. The way her bulging white disc-like eyes seem to dilate while her small black pupils shrink puts me on edge. The longer I gaze back at her, the more everything else in the world seems to fade into blackness and her eyes only get wider and whiter until her face distorts and stretches from the size difference and then her eyes start to bend and become uneven with each other and the top of her head extends upward and then curls over her ear while the skin in her face shrivels and bends over itself again and again in overlapping flaps as her head continues to distort into a spiral—

2:37 AM. I look away and head back into the kitchen for my sleeping pills. Now that the worst is almost over, it's time to get ready for some much-needed sleep. In three hours, I'll have some repairs to make. I take two Melatonin capsules and wash them down with another mouthful of beer. Then I dump the last third of my bottle down the drain and drop the bottle in. It clatters loudly against the stainless steel walls of the sink.

Another *thunk* from behind the living room wall opposite my position. It's muffled and it's followed by a dull ratcheting sound. She couldn't have raised the garage doors, could she?

Back to the knife set. Once again, I take out the chef's knife and head through the dining room through the screen door into the fridge area. There's a light scraping at the door to the rear deck but I know that's not what I heard. The sound I heard came from the garage. I check the door knob. The button is pushed in, indicating that it's locked. I press my ear up against the door and try to drown out all noise from the deck, straining to hear anything, *anything* that may be moving around in the garage. For a while, all I can hear is the scratching behind me. The room gets darker and I turn to see Maureen's face pressed up against the small window, saucer-like eyes stabbing me with manic hatred. I turn and reach up into the pantry above the chest freezer and bring down an unopened box of cereal and squeeze it into the slit in front of the glass, blocking my view of her and more importantly, *her* view of me.

"Let me see my children," she whimpers. "Cameron? Cameron?"

"Go away."

"Let me see them. You can't take my children from me!"

"They're not your children."

"Yes, they are!" she cries. "They're *mine* and you can't keep me away from them!"

"Fuck off!" I snarl.

"Cameron!" She slaps her palms on the window and moans in heartbroken agony—a tactic that has lost its desired effect long ago, when I wasn't as smart as I am now. I stand there, staring at the cereal box until the slapping ceases and the moans trail off. Then I heave a sigh and press my ear against the garage door again.

I hear *something* sliding around in there. I imagine a giant slug pushing a sandbag across the concrete floor. God, I would take a giant slug over what's probably in there any day of the goddamn week. Opening the door would be risky. We're at the edge of her window. Should I wait until after three, when her powers have weakened even more? The pills are starting to take effect on my eyelids. I blink, feeling my eyes burn with fatigue.

Go to bed, Cameron. Go to bed, man. It's not worth it. Think of the kids. Knife or no knife, it's not worth it.

Something *thuds* in there and I know that my car was just bludgeoned by a dull instrument of some kind, or perhaps it was hit with a fist...

Just go to bed. The car doesn't fucking work anyway. She cut the brake line, remember? Just imagine if you hadn't noticed the fluid before you got in and started driving the damn thing. You wouldn't be a father anymore, would you, Cameron? Hell, without brakes, you probably wouldn't be alive enough to care what happened to them anyway, would you?

Just shut up. I get it. The door is locked already. Why risk it? She'll find her way in eventually. No matter what I do to beef up security in this fucking house, the bitch always finds a way in, doesn't she?

Yes, she does...

So I return inside and check the kids' locks one final time and then I go to my room and shut the door. I strip into my underwear and climb into bed and lie there in the dark room lit by dark blue slits leaking through the boards over the window. The ceiling swirls above me and before I know it I'm not staring at the ceiling, I'm staring at my closed eyelids.

The wall stares at me with empty black pits that seem to lead straight down into another world. Or maybe it's the floor and I'm standing on the wall... I don't feel the pull of gravity here, nor do I see anything else except the blue light that swirls and pulsates across the interior of this strange little room. The pits flicker and shift slightly in my direction. Another, larger opening gapes beneath them. "Enter me," it says, and I do, like always. My obedience takes me to a black room with no light, void of feeling, of sensation. No sound could be heard, not even my own. I try to scream but my mouth is gone. My arms and legs feel like lead and suddenly I realize I'm not walking, I'm *floating*. An invisible, shapeless force carries me further into the hole, deeper into the abyss, and I'm strapped in for the ride whether I like it or not. I suck in air and I scream without a mouth again. Falling, endless falling.

And then all movement stops. I touch solid ground. I look down at the floor and I can see hell beneath its clear surface—a darkness that does not entirely conceal whatever dwells within it. Shapes writhe and contort under my feet. Hands press themselves up against the floor, trying to push through. I stagger and look around for an exit. Nothing but black walls all around me, closing in.

A figure, tall and slender, rises from the floor like a wax statue melting in reverse; a fluid mass at first before adopting a parody of a human shape. It looks *almost* human, but something about it just *isn't*.

"Where are the children?" someone asks. "Are they safe?"

My mouth is back and it says, "Yes."

"Are you *sure*?"

The bow-like figure in front of me quivers. A featureless oval propped on a slender, twisted branch coils around. Each movement makes a wet crunching sound.

"Where are the children?"

"They're safe," I assure it, though I'm more-or-less assuring myself more than it. Whatever *it* is.

SHE WATCHES ME BURY HER

The abstract being shivers again, and then it expands like the sail of a great medieval galley, flooding my vision with its thin, wide mass. A multitude of eyes snap open across its face and they all look at me with strange indifference.

"Give me my children."

"Wake up."

A distortion of Maureen stands at the foot of my bed, stretched high enough to graze the ceiling with the stray hairs extending from her blood-darkened head. Her eyes, pearly white and fixed on me with a piercing gaze. Her arms at her sides. Her naked body is misshapen, lifelessly grey despite the navy blue shade of early morning coming through the boards in narrow stripes, patterning her long torso.

I'm paralyzed, staring at her with half-sleep. If this were the first time I'd seen her like this, I would be wide awake. I know that she cannot hurt me. My heart pounds, dragging me out of sleep, and a feeling of dread creeps up my spine. She's *in* the house now, but what about the others? How many more found their way inside?

Now I'm wide awake. "Maureen," I stutter.

"Where are my children?" she rasps.

"Safe," I reply.

"Where are they?"

"They are safe."

"I want to see them."

"You can't."

"I have to see my children."

"No," I say softly, "you don't."

Her eyes flare with anger. Her arms bend and her tendril-fingers rise into my view, bending at the joints, rigid with barely contained fury. They're much shorter now than they were before. "You *will* let me see my children..."

I fight to keep my breath steady and my own temper down. "Like *hell* I will, you evil little *bitch*."

She moans like a wounded animal, rising in volume until it hurts my ears and shakes the entire house. She shrieks, now, and flails her arms wildly, tendril-fingers sweeping picture frames off the dresser drawer and striking the bed's footboard. Then she latches all of her fingers onto the footboard and pulls it forward and backward while her screaming head lurches with such violence that the likelihood of it flying off her shoulders seems entirely possible. The bed rocks with her, threatening to come apart, and I lie there with my hands gripping the sheets and the headboard smacking my skull.

Then she releases the bed and takes her anger out on the door, grabbing the knobs on both sides and screeching and yanking the hinges right out in her final show of strength. The door falls to the floor and, panting, wheezing; Maureen's disfigurements begin to fade as she crumples to the floor in a sad heap. Her inhuman height begins to diminish. My wife *shrinks* before my eyes, shrivelling back into the barely six-foot woman I married a long time ago. Her black hair is dishevelled and hangs over her face like a wet mop head.

I glance at the digital clock on the bedside table. 5:59 AM. Relief washes over me. It's over. I look at her again and I see the light peach colour in her skin returning and there isn't a single cut or scrape on her body; not a streak of dried blood or the slightest discolouration that would indicate any kind of abuse. If I told someone I killed her just hours ago, they would think I was just telling a bad joke.

"Come back to bed, Maureen."

Slowly she does, crawling along the side of the bed and then slipping into it, still crying. She slinks into my arms. Her skin is cold and I notice she's trembling feverishly. She sobs into my chest and I hold her tightly and run my fingers through her soft hair and I shush her every time she gasps and crackles in sorrow, and I tell her everything's gonna be alright.

"I'm sorry," she whimpers. "I'm sorry, I'm so, so sorry."

"Shh," I whisper, and she nestles her head under my chin. "You have nothing to be afraid of." I blink back tears of my own as my heart starts to break all over again. "I'll protect you."

SHE WATCHES ME BURY HER

Part Three: Saturday, October 21st, 2000

6:21 AM. Maureen sleeps soundly and I leave her tucked in under the covers. I don't get dressed and get to work in my underwear. The door is the first thing I get to work on. It takes me a good twenty minutes to get it back in its frame, albeit a little crooked. Nothing I can do about that now; she's twisted the damn thing so often that it's gotten warped from all the abuse.

6:45 AM. I unlock the kids' doors and leave them ajar so that they know they're not locked in when they wake up, and then I check the bathroom, which looks clean and ordinary, just as I'd left it. I check the basement next and it's exactly how I left it, too. I remember the rat and take a glue trap down from an overhead cupboard and fit it in the corner where the hole is. Then I go back upstairs. The front door isn't smashed in, though I make a mental note that the screen door is probably ruined. The kitchen, living room, dining area and pool room all seem to be okay. The windows and doors aren't broken. I look at the garage doorknob. The button is out, which means somehow, at some point, Maureen found a way to unlock it.

But *how*? She's not a locksmith. She's not a career criminal. Hell, maybe she's an expert when it comes to breaking and entering, since she keeps finding a way in and I keep scratching my head wondering how the fuck she managed to do it. Guess I married Houdini.

I remember hearing something weird in here, so I push the lock in, whatever good that does anymore, and I grab the chef's knife out of the block, and then I return to the garage door and open it. A pool of blood in front of my car curves around to the driver's side in a series of jagged smears that end under the door. My eyes flick up at the face behind the windshield, which has been reduced to a glistening sheet of diamond lacework, caved in bloody handprints.

Brandishing the knife, I hurry down the steps, shutting the door behind me, and peer into the driver side window at Maureen's sleeping face, her head craned back against the seat. She managed to get her blood all over the seats and the dash and the windows while she was in there. Thinking of escaping in *this* car? I have to scoff. Good luck with that. After she cut the brake line, I emptied the tank in a jerry can and locked it away.

She's still asleep, or she's pretending. I'll find out soon enough.

I open the door and it creaks loudly. She doesn't stir. Keeping my eyes on her, I stoop down and push the button under the wheel to pop the trunk. *Now* she shifts, slightly, and I plunge the knife into her throat.

Her eyes pop open and bulge in terror. She convulses, tries to pry the knife out of her neck, but I keep it there and grimace when her fingernails slice into my hand. She looks at me, tears streaming down her face, horror bleeding from those big brown eyes of hers. The knife tip cuts into the headrest's leather. She gurgles. Blood bubbles from the corners of her mouth and drips onto my hand. I look away, listening to her choke on the blood.

Finally she stops resisting and slumps against the seat. I lift her out of the car, cradling her like a sleeping child, and put her in the trunk. With the knife in my hand, I slam the trunk down and head for the door, shoving the driver side door shut on my way out. I'm careful to keep my bloody hands from leaving too much of a mess as I make my way into the kitchen. There, I clean the knife and wash my hands. My chest is saturated pink with my wife's blood, so I take a shower.

7:32 AM. By the time I'm out of the shower, dressed, teeth brushed, the works; the kids are up and watching *Transformers* in the living room. One look at them and I know they didn't get much sleep last night. Maybe they didn't get any and they heard everything that went on…

"Morning, kiddos," I say as cheerfully as possible.

They barely acknowledge my presence. Optimus Prime orders his Autobots to roll out on the TV.

"Hungry?"

No response.

"I'll make some bacon and eggs. How's that sound?"

They're as lifeless as statues.

I sigh and head into the kitchen to make them breakfast. I can't stand to look at them anymore. I can't imagine what this is all doing to them. They used to be bright, cheerful, hyper-active little hellions that no one could control. Now they don't do anything and barely say anything. They've been reduced to mindless drones and it kills me every day when I look into their sunken little eyes. Three years since this all started; their faces have aged ten.

8:01 AM. Three layers of freshly cooked bacon strips lie stacked in paper towel sheets on a plate while I shovel the kids' scrambled eggs onto their plates with a spatula. "Come and get it."

The kids file in and silently take their plates. "Grab some bacon," I say. "As much as you like." They heed my words without a sound, selecting two, three, or five strips off the plate, and then take their seats around the dining room table. I join them with my own plate at the head of the table in front of the window that faces the shed, stealing a quick sweeping glance outside before I sit down. I don't see any other copies of her roaming around outside. I'll have to be more thorough when I finish breakfast.

I turn back to the kids and watch them mechanically shove food in their mouths and chew with their mouths closed, staring at the table with dull expressions. I can feel another dull, hot pang in my chest. "Mary."

Mary stops eating to look at me.

"How's uh… how's junior kindergarten?"

"Senior."

"What?"

"I'm in senior kindergarten," she says quietly.

"Oh." Of course, you idiot. You're really losing it now, aren't you? "How's senior kindergarten?"

She shrugs and starts eating again.

I nod slowly. If she doesn't want to talk, she doesn't want to talk. Can't force her to do something she doesn't want to do. "Todd? How's school?"

Todd keeps eating. Doesn't even acknowledge my presence. Okay.

"Michael?"

Michael looks at me and I can see fear in his eyes. Suddenly he's paralyzed. The only thing moving is his trembling hand holding his fork.

"Are you okay?" I ask him, eyeing him carefully, looking for any obvious signs of sickness. "You're shaking."

He bolts suddenly, fork clattering on his plate. "Michael!" I call out to him, but he's already gone back to the living room.

Todd looks at me and then stands up, takes his plate and

follows him at a more even pace. He pauses in the entryway and glances at Mary, who climbs down from her chair, takes her plate off the table, and exits with her eldest, leaving me alone.

I stare at me plate and start to choke on my own tears and swallow it down instead. Don't cry, you fuck. It's what she wants. Don't cry. Don't give her that power. I can feel my eyes start to water and hastily wipe them on my sleeve. Appetite's gone now. I dump my plate in the bin and throw my plate in the sink and check on the kids to make sure they're accounted for. All three of them are on the couch staring at that damn TV.

8:18 AM. I have a screen door to fix—*if* I can even fix it. With my toolbox, I step out on the ramp to assess the damage and find that yes, she tore it off its hinges, and now it's folded across the ramp's banister with a smashed window, and the screen mesh is all shredded.

Can't fix this problem today. I would need to buy a new door, and for what? For her to break it again? No thanks. We'll have to live without a screen door. What a goddamn *tragedy*.

I lift the screen door and drag it out to the shed—

Oh, shit.

Its door's hanging wide open when I step round the corner and it makes me drop the broken door in a heartbeat. I run up the steps and look inside. The fresh coat of blood I painted the interior with last night has mostly dried up. A few small pools remain in the corners and under the bench. I look at the door's splintered frame, now missing its lock. I thought it'd be strong enough. Guess I was wrong. She never targeted the shed before. Guess she was a little pissed about the methods I utilized last—

The chainsaw. Christ, *where is the chainsaw*?

Leaping into the shed, I frantically search for it. How could I have been so fucking stupid?! Of *course* she would take it! Of course! My eyes dart across each shelf and then flick up at the rafters in the ceiling and then I drop to my knees and scan beneath the bench but it's gone, it's fucking gone; she took the fucking chainsaw! "Shit. Shit. Shit. *Shit. Shit. SHIT!*" Panic, fear, anger, you name it, it's surging through my body so fast I don't even realize I'm kicking the bench over until it's already done. I scream at the top of my lungs, every profanity in the book until my vocal cords start to burn, flailing around like I've just lost my mind and maybe I *have* lost it, tossing things around, smashing up pans and bins and hurling tools against the wall until a goddamned mallet bounces back and bites the back of my right hand and I shout again, this time in pain. I slump down the wall and I almost cry again but I stop myself this time, too.

And then I hear the unmistakable drone of an engine coming up the driveway…

8:27 AM. A police patrol car rolls up in front of the garage and I'm down the front path faster than lightning to meet the patrolman before both of his feet can touch the concrete. The driver's side door slams shut and I glimpse a familiar face under the wide-brimmed hat behind the cherries. He came alone, I think; I can't see anyone else in the car.

Constable Henry Jameson glides around the front end of his patrol car with the kind of grace one might find in a dancer rather than a cop. Matter of fact, I've seen Henry dance. It's one of his many talents. He regards me with a nod and doesn't try to hide the concerned expression on his round face. "Cameron."

"Morning, Henry." Despite my outburst I manage to keep myself looking relatively composed. "What can I do for you?"

He approaches me, glances at the house, narrowing his eyes at the boards over the windows like it's the first time he's seen them. "Still uh… still not feeling well?"

"No," I reply.

"How're the kids?"

"Kids're fine."

He looks at me. Eyes shaded under his hat. "You missing something, Cameron?"

I squint. Something's definitely wrong. "What do you mean?"

He turns, opens the rear passenger door. Inside is a green blanket rumpled up across the seats with two mud-caked feet poking out from underneath. He helps his passenger up and out of the car and my heart sinks when I see another familiar face partially concealed under the blanket, which she holds together like a cloak. She's pale and shivering. A few clumsy slips opens a few gaps in her blanket, revealing nothing but flesh underneath.

"Maureen," I gasp. My whole body goes stiff but my heart drums faster than it should.

Henry shuts the door behind her and turns to face me. "Found her roaming in the ditch about two kilometres from here. She uh," he chuckles quietly and runs his thumbnail back and forth across his forehead. "She wasn't wearing anything, Cameron."

As if in a daze, Maureen closes the gap between us and presses her face against my chest. She's cold and damp; hair's a stringy wet mess. I wrap my arms around her and keep her close.

Henry continues, "Took her down to the station and she snapped out of it, I guess. We didn't have a change of clothes anywhere—shame on us, I know—we had a blanket. That was about it. Damn-near gave Roland a heart attack."

"Still works there, does he?"

"That old bastard won't ever retire."

"Where'd you find her?"

"Like I said, couple kilometres," Henry says. "Out by the cemetery. Know why she would go by there?"

"Why?"

"I'm asking you."

"Oh." I think up a story and fast: "She's been sleepwalking lately. She never left the house before, I-I uh… I don't know what compelled her to do that."

"Yeah, that's what we figured. She didn't remember a thing about what she was doing. Not like we can charge a sleepwalker for indecent exposure, right?" He snickers good-naturedly. "She insisted she was okay and wanted to go home. Seemed fine to us. Not like she had any injuries or anything. Wasn't acting scared or threatened." He shrugged. "So here we are."

"I'm sorry about this, Henry."

"Hey, don't worry about it. No harm done."

"I don't know what else to say."

"Well," Henry says with a friendly grin, "next time you guys go to bed, try to remember some clothes. No telling what the neighbours might think. Any of the four or five of them scattered out here." He laughs. "Hell, we wouldn't want to kill Roland, would we?"

"Or *would* we?" I chuckle dryly.

He laughs. "He's been a bit mellower since you left. Speaking of… when're you coming back? Station misses you, we all do."

"Just gotta sort some stuff out, Henry. I'm sorry it's taking so long."

"Man's gotta do what a man's gotta do. Take all the time you need. Just know that, uh, we're getting impatient." He gives me a sad smile. "Get some sleep. You look like shit."

Same old Henry. I reply, "An improvement over what you saw in the mirror this morning, huh?"

"Ah, fuck you," Henry says, laughing again. "Not a chance. I gotta go." He heads back around his car and climbs in behind the wheel. The passenger window rolls down and he yells through it, "Take care of your lady there, buddy. Hope I see you soon!"

Still holding Maureen against me, I wave him goodbye as he backs his patrol car down the driveway. I wait until he's back on the road driving behind the trees before I hold Maureen out and take another look at her. It's her, it's *really* her. The resemblance is beyond uncanny. She even *smells* like her. But it isn't, is it? The real Maureen is sleeping soundly in our bed. Right? Or is *that* the copy? Which Maureen is real? *Which one*?

Does it matter? They're *all* her; they're all Maureen, aren't they? And they're *all* afflicted; *they* can't die, either, like this one or the one in the bedroom or the others that may be wandering around in the forest or roadside ditches or the cemetery, the goddamn *cemetery* of all places—

I look at her face, which is smeared with dirt and mud. "Maureen." Her head lolls sleepily to the side. She's dozing in my arms so I shake her to wake her up. "Maureen!"

Her eyes snap open again and she looks at me in utter bewilderment. I ask her, "Where did you take the chainsaw?"

She gives me a blank stare.

"Where is it? Where's the chainsaw? Where did you put it?"

No response. I feel her put more weight against my arms as her legs start to give out. She's succumbing to her fatigue. Guess this one never slept. I shake her again, rocking her head backward and forward. She's like a ragdoll in my arms. "Answer me, goddamn you!"

Still nothing, but I sense recognition in her eyes. The bitch knows what I'm talking about and she's refusing to give in. She's planning something and she refuses to tell me what it is or how she's going to go about it with her copycat pals, the other Maureens, when night comes along again and it starts all over again.

I start down the path, towing her by the wrist. She staggers and stumbles trying to keep up with my pace, losing her blanket along the way, too tired to pick it up or cry out. I yank her in front of the shed and direct her head so that she can see into it, at the tools scattered across the floor and the upturned work bench. "You and the others broke in, you *broke* in. Look at the door. The lock's gone, right? Where's the lock? Where's the fucking *chainsaw*? What'd you do with it?"

"I don't know, I don't know what you're—"

I shove her up the stairs and throw her onto the tools. Now she's scared, making a real theatrical show of hysterics, scrambling to the other end of the shed and curling up in the corner. I shut the door behind me—like it does me a lot of good now—and I shout, "WHERE'S THE FUCKING CHAINSAW!"

"I don't know!" she screams. Tears stream down her face. Stop it, not now, not *this* now. It's not even fucking noon and I'm already—

I pick up the mallet and approach her. "Where... where is it? *Where?*"

She's so confused, so harmless...

Now you know that's a lie, don't you? You know that's a lie and you know you know it. It's all a farce, just a play to make you feel bad.

"*Where is it?*"

"I don't know, I don't know, what do you want from me—"

That's when I start using the mallet.

9:12 AM is when I finally step out of the shed into the sunlight and I stop on the first step to take it in and breathe, just *breathe* in that crisp morning air. My wet clothes are sticking to me, some areas dried faster than others and now they're rubbing irritably against my skin and it makes me shiver. I crane my neck and see a sparkling gold-and-blue sky; it's blurred behind a twinkling, shifting mass of octagonal patterns... oh. I'm crying. I gave in. That's it. I fall on the steps and I listen to the birds singing in the trees and I bawl my eyes out under the sun's warm glare. Every heartbeat feels like a red-hot poker driving its way through my chest and burning me from the inside out. The tears sting my eyes. They're hot as they stream down my face. I let her win this time. I gave in.

9:32 AM. I pull myself together as best as I can before I set out to clean up the mess Maureen and I made last night. The lawn chair's fucked worse than the screen door, so I discard it behind the shed next to a stack of mouldy old boxes with broken lock clasps and splintered lids. I return to the patio and catch a few dark red streaks that weren't there before and sigh. I have my work cut out for me today. Gotta clean up all the gore and find out where that bitch took the chainsaw to.

I run a lap around the pool, glancing into the forest, peering under the pool table in the water, and when I reach the edge of the hole the multitude of Maureens crawled out of I look into it, too. Nowhere. Next I check the deck's diagonal crosshatched skirting, peeking through the diamonds into the hollow beneath the floorboards at mounds of dirt and piled rocks. Nothing. I stand up straight and look around at the tall, slender trees swaying in the wind all around the house. Christ, it could be *anywhere* out there in the bush, swallowed by an ocean of fallen leaves and tangled branches.

9:45 AM. I put my mind to a different task for the moment: the body in the shed. I pull two garbage bags out of a drawer in the kitchen and take them out to the shed. Once there, I curl the body into a fetal position and roll her clumsily into one of the bags and then close that bag up with a couple of tight knots before stretching the second bag over the first and closing that one similar to the first. Now where the hell do I put it? Once the witching hour strikes, she'll claw her way out in no time. Lock her in the trunk of my car with the other one? No… but what else is the damn thing good for?

But then she'll be in the house. Once the witching hour strikes, they'll both spring back to life in the trunk of that car and then they'll get the garage door open and there will be hell to pay. For now, all I can do is leave her out here.

And that's exactly what I do—I toss the bag behind the shelf on top of the broken lawn chair, and then I fetch two more bags from the kitchen and gather the other dead Maureen from the trunk of my car into the double-layer of plastic and I toss her behind the shed, too. Starting to look like a real dump back here now.

When I head back toward the house, I see Todd step out onto the deck and approach the edge of the pool. He looks beyond the pool into the trees and holds his stare for a few seconds before sitting himself down and looking over at me. I wave at him. He looks away, expressionless, and stares at the forest again. I cross the patio and ascend the steps and go around to his left. "Hey."

No response.

"Mind of I sit here?"

He shrugs.

"If you don't want me to, I won't."

He speaks for the first time in days: "It's okay." My heart skips; genuinely startled. The kid has a soft voice, gentle and airy.

I sit down and look at the forest next to him. Now what? What do I say to him? *"Hey, how you doin'?"* *"How about those riots in Israel a few weeks ago, huh, son? Wild."* Christ. For a while I just sit there next to my son trying to think up some kind of conversation starter. What do I say to a nine-year-old in this situation?

Then I think of something that isn't the ideal conversation starter, but something that should be addressed all the same: "Where're your brother and sister?"

"Still watching TV."

I nod. "Your mom up yet?"

"No."

"Okay."

More silence. We're perched on eggshells here. The white noise of the rustling leaves fills our ears and the cool breeze caresses us under the sun's gentle warmth.

"Dad..."

"Yeah?"

"Can I..."

I look at him and he looks away. "What is it, son?"

He hesitates further.

"Todd, you can ask me anything. You know that, right?"

"I don't know if I can."

"What do you mean?"

"What if you start hitting me like you hit mom?"

Well, that stings, but I can't blame him for thinking like that. It still hurts, and so I try to say something to make him understand in a way that makes sense, in a way that makes him stop fearing me, in a way that doesn't turn him or Mary or Michael against their own mother. My mouth hangs open but no explanation comes out. Nothing, not a sound. Eventually I shut my mouth. "I would never hurt you, Todd..."

"I don't believe you."

"I know you don't," I mutter, unable to hide the sadness in my voice. "I know what it looks like. Trust me, I do. I know what it looks like to you. I understand your fear, kiddo. I get it. It's… *complicated*."

"Why is everything so complicated with adults?"

"Not *everything*. Some things. Most things. Uh, a lot of things. S-sometimes it's very straightforward, and other times, it's, it's strangely complicated. This… this is one of those things."

"But when I asked why Buster ran away, you didn't *really* answer."

"What'd I say?"

"You said it was complicated. I guess I kinda knew you would say that *this* is complicated, too. Don't know why I bothered asking."

"Todd, you have every right to ask."

"What's the point when you don't answer?"

"Because I have that right, too."

He gives me a frustrated glare. "Why?"

"To protect you."

"That's bullshit."

"Hey, now. Language."

"Stop holding my hand, dad."

"Huh?"

"Do you think I don't hear things? Do you think Michael and I just *magically* fall asleep when we go to bed? We hear things, dad. We hear mom screaming outside of our windows and we hear her trying to break in and sometimes… sometimes she *talks* to us." He breaks down, blubbering over his rigid hands. His voice cracks when he adds, "Why? Why are you doing this?"

He shudders beside me and I watch him in my own helpless, stupid way. I have no idea how to calm him. Nothing he says surprises me, but watching his mask of stoic calmness dissolving before my eyes does everything except physically kill me. "What does she say to you?"

He sniffles and wipes his nose on his jacket. Glazed red eyes look pitifully at me. "All kinds of stuff."

"Like what?"

"You know… she wants us to let her in. She… she wants us to help her. I can't even sleep anymore, dad. When I sleep, all I see is mom, but the… the…"

He trembles again, squeaking as he tries to take a breath

uninterrupted by his crying. "Whatever that *thing* I keep seeing out there is, it... it *isn't* mom, it's..."

"Something else."

"What's going on? Is that really mom? *Our* mom? What does it want?"

I heave a deep sigh. "I wish I could tell you, Todd."

"Why can't you?"

"Because," I say, and I can't help but scoff before I tell him, "I don't know what it is, either. But you have to understand: it's *not* your mother. That thing you see outside isn't her. It *looks* like her and it *sounds* like her and it knows everything she knows about you but it's *not* her and you have to understand that you can't, under *any* circumstances, let her in the house. Do you understand me?"

"Why? What's going on?"

"Just promise me you won't let that thing in the house. Don't even open the window. Don't unlock the door. Don't take the boards off the windows. Don't do *anything* that makes its entry all the more possible."

"Dad, *please*."

I inhale deeply and take my time to exhale, trying to keep myself calm.

"Is it mom?"

"No," I lie—or do I? Honestly, I can't figure it out myself. *Is* that thing Maureen, or is it really just some demonic *thing* that looks like her? "No, it isn't her. If it was, do you think she'd be in bed every morning? Look at my shirt, Todd." I point at my shirt and turn my body toward him so he can see the fresh blood spatters on it from the interrogation I'd conducted in the shed. "Do you remember how white this shirt was? Now look at it."

Todd's eyes, disturbed by the stark red streaks and blots, flick up and down and side to side at my shirt. They're wide, fearful.

"Your mom's sleeping in her room. Meanwhile, I'm out here, still keeping that thing from coming inside. That's all I've been doing, Todd. That's it. That's all."

I catch a brief flash of mild relief on Todd's face, like this was some kind of revelation that introduced an entirely new concept to his growing mind. "I guess not," he says thoughtfully.

"It's not her, Todd. It's something that *looks* like her. I... I wouldn't hit anyone if I didn't think it was justified. Trust me. I was a cop, you know."

"I know," he says quietly, sniffling.

We sit there for a time, watching the pool's bright blue tarp collect leaves. Todd asks, "What *is* it?"

"What is what?"

"The thing that looks like mom?"

And I think about what the hell it *could* be. Is it a witch? A demon? Spiritual possession? Was this goddamned house built on an ancient Indian burial ground? Is God himself punishing me? Hell, I don't know. She still eats salty foods and a stake through her heart doesn't have any lasting effect, either. She defies every rule I know of, be it religious, supernatural, or mythological—the rules I've had the resources to enforce, at least. I don't have access to holy water, for instance; I don't have silver bullets nor do I know of any methods to obtain any around here. How do I stop her? How do I get it to leave? And if it leaves, will she die once it leaves?

"I wish I knew," I answer him.

10:37 AM. Todd and I head inside and I ask him if he has any homework. "No," he says.

"Alright. I have to do some cleaning. If you need me, just yell."

"Okay." And away he goes. My oldest son, brave in his own way, and smart, too. He disappears into the kitchen and I hear his feet walk across the living room floor. The springs in the couch groan as he assumes his place on it.

I step into the garage and look at my battered car and its crystallized windshield, and all the blood smearing the interior and the puddle drying on the floor. For the next hour or so, I'm scrubbing every red surface until the blood is faded a very light pink or wiped away completely. The garage's concrete floor is a different story. The puddle sits atop the dark spot I scrubbed yesterday. I shred a sponge on the damn thing until there's just a slightly darker and now wider stain on the floor. By the time I'm done, I'm perspired, breathing heavy, and my arms hurt so bad they're trembling beyond my control. "Shit," I mutter.

11:58 AM. After another shower, I dispose of my bloodied clothes in favour of a black sweater and black track pants, and then double-check everything in the house to make damn sure it's secure and nothing else is out of place. Both sides of the house are fine.

The boards over the kids' windows have plenty more claw marks than yesterday, with one board having been ripped off of Mary's window and tossed into the grass not far from the path. I fetch a hammer and nails and replace it immediately. The sides of the house are fine. The trampled garden and the broken birdbath haven't been altered. I even walk along the edge of the property, looking into the woods for any sign of the chainsaw, but I don't find it. That makes me nervous. I can feel this horrible dread reaching down and gripping me, holding me in place for what I strongly suspect will be one hell of a terrible night. I pray it'll be like the time the cleaver disappeared and was never seen again, perhaps hoarded by her, or a copy of her before forgetting where she put it. Christ, I can only guess what she'll do once she finds it…

I try not to think about it as I head inside and fix the kids lunch. Grilled cheese sandwiches. When the food's ready, I summon them to the table and they seem a bit more relaxed than they were this morning. Todd must've relayed the information I gave him.

Michael lifts his sandwich off his plate and looks at me. "Thanks, dad."

I look at him, stunned. Then I reply with, "You're welcome, Michael."

Mary smiles at me and it makes me want to hug her and never let her go. One step at a time, Cameron. One step at a time.

12:22 PM. We're halfway through our meal when Maureen walks in, clad in a pink nightgown. She looks utterly exhausted and barely able to keep her eyes open. "Good morning," she moans.

The kids hesitate to respond. "Afternoon," I say to her.

Her half-open eyes fall on the children and her face lights up in a loving smile that I know is all too genuine. "My sweethearts." She reaches for Michael. He recoils slightly but she doesn't seem to notice and places her hand on his head, tousling his hair. Michael glances worriedly at me and I give him a reassuring look that calms him down a little. "I'm sorry I slept in so late. Grilled cheese! Yummy."

I offer my services while she's still in a good mood: "I can make you some."

"Thank you." She takes her seat at the opposite end of the table between Michael and Todd, making them stiffen. "I'd love some." She gives me a grateful smile. An 'I'm lucky to have you' smile. I know it won't last. It never does.

Still, I get up, uneasy with the idea of leaving her alone with the kids, even *if* it's the middle of the day. I periodically peek in while I prepare her grilled cheese sandwiches. As soon as they finish I bring them to her on a plate post-haste and reclaim my spot with my back to the window that faces the shed. I watch her and I think about how happy she looks when the children are among the first things she sees when she wakes up. The joyful twinkle in her eyes when she strokes their heads and plays games with them and nurtures them chokes me up and I have to look away and pretend everything's alright for a few hours more.

The last half of my second sandwich remains uneaten. My appetite died when she walked in the room.

1:29 PM. Todd follows me out into the backyard by the pit in the ground and bends forward with his hands on his knees, looking into it. I have my back turned to him, taking another shot in my search for the chainsaw. This time I venture into the woods, careful not to walk too far out of range of the house. Todd follows me and is silent for a while as I kick up leaves and move loose brush around just in case she's hidden it under them. I straighten my back and scan the forest floor hopelessly, looking over the endless sea of crumpled, dry leaves that cover the earth in their fiery collage of autumn colours. She picked the perfect season to pull this shit.

"Why do you bother, dad?"

"What do you mean?" I ask, continuing my search with him behind me.

"Why do you bury her after you kill her? Or *it*. Or whatever. I mean, it just comes right back, right?"

"Slows her down."

"It does?"

"Definitely."

"Why, though?"

"Why, what?"

"Does it really slow her down a lot?"

"About half an hour, normally. Sometimes an hour, depending on various circumstances."

"Like what?"

Patience, Cameron. Kids are curious things. He has every

right to be asking questions. Hell, you should be rejoicing. He's said more to you today than he has all month. That's a goddamn miracle all on its own. Your children aren't as far out of the loop now as they were before. Isn't that a good thing?

Isn't it?

"Well... you know... lots of things. Things you're better off not knowing."

"I can take it."

"It's not exactly a matter of whether or not you can take it, son."

"Huh?"

"I'm more concerned about you knowing too much about it. There's a reason I didn't give you or your siblings any details on what was going on with your mother and I."

"What is it?"

"You're relentless today, aren't you?" I shake my head at myself, hoping my tone doesn't sound too serious as to offend him. "Whatever that thing is that comes out is still your mother."

"*Is* she?"

"During the day she is, yes."

"What about at night? What is she?"

"I don't know."

"You know what I think?"

"What?"

"She turns into a banshee or something. Or a witch."

"A banshee," I repeat blandly, "a witch." She's none of those things. I know that. She screams at night—boy, does she scream—but that's as far as the similarities go.

I know I didn't marry a witch, either. I would've noticed something a whole lot sooner if she was.

"Is that why you lock us in our rooms? You don't want us to see the witch?"

"She's not a witch."

"How do you know?"

"Of course I would know," I state a little sharper than originally intended. "I *married* her."

"Then—?"

"Let me tell you something," I interrupt him, turning to face him. He bumps into me and takes a step back, looking alarmed. I lay it to him straight: "I can't possibly explain whatever's going on here myself, okay? I'm not an expert. I'm not a genius. Every possible solution I've ever heard of from movies, books, the radio, the... *goddamn Bible* haven't worked worth shit on that thing. Believe me, I *looked*, and you damn well better believe I *tried... everything!*" I'm shouting now that I'm going off on a tangent: "And I know she wasn't like that before I met her or after I married her, or even after she had Mary, because none of this insane bullshit happened until *after* we moved to this fucking house! You wanna help? You know what you can do to help? Todd, I'm asking you a question. You know *my* father taught me? It's simple. It's unbeatable. So far it's worked wonders. You know what that is?"

Todd looks small in his growing fear. Something tells me he's kicking himself for following me out here. "What?" he asks.

"'Don't break the routine.' That's what he said. 'Don't break the routine.' Todd, I-I don't know how to stop it or how to kill it or how to keep it contained, but if there's anything I *do* know it's all the stuff I've managed to work into a routine. This routine works. You break the routine, you're fucked. Not *me*, I'll be fine from a physical standpoint; Todd, I mean you, *you* will be fucked, Todd; and not just *you*, but Michael and Mary, too. I can't, under *any* circumstances, allow her to get into your rooms. But I know what you see and hear when she calls you in the middle of the night, when she talks to you through the windows, Todd. I know she looks like your mother and she sounds like your mother, but *trust* me, Todd— Todd, you listening? Look at me, Todd. Look—yes, at me. Not at the forest. The trees can't save you, Todd. The trees can't save you, and without those locked doors, neither can I. I wouldn't blame you kids if you opened your doors and let her in—after all, she looks and sounds and smells like your mother, but trust me, *trust* me, Todd, you gotta trust me on this: when the sun isn't up, when it's dark between the hours of midnight to six in the morning, she's *not* your mom. You think I lock you in your rooms out of paranoia, or, or because I enjoy it? No! No, never. But I know how manipulative she can be, Todd, and I know that even though you're smart kids, you're still kids, and kids are stupid, and it's that stupidity that would get you killed if it weren't for those locks. You understand me, Todd?"

"Yes." Todd nods his head furiously.

"*Do* you? Do you really?"

"Dad, please."

"What? *What?*"

"You're scaring me." He glances into the forest and then looks back at me.

That's right, Cameron. Cool it. Simmer down. Just a kid. Just a kid. You're gonna drive them away again if you act crazy like that. Just breathe—that's it, breathe. You're getting too emotional again. You're running on two goddamn hours of sleep, Cameron.

I fall to my knees so that my face is level with his and I'm panting, exhausted by my own outburst and my lack of sleep. My heart races and the tears start to flow again as I reach for him. He pulls away for a moment, and I figure he's not exactly in a hugging mood, so I touch his shoulders instead, as lightly as possible so he knows he can leave if he chooses. I look him in the eyes and I tell him, "I'm sorry, Todd. That was... that was a little intense. It's been a long couple of years."

"Dad." He tries to turn his head away but I reposition it so that his face is parallel with mine. His eyes, however, are uncooperative, still looking at the forest behind me to the far left.

"I couldn't stand to lose you guys, Todd. I want you to have a future and grow up and have families of your own, hopefully without—"

Todd staggers out of my reach, fear distorting his features. "Dad!"

I swivel toward the direction he's looking and I see Maureen peeking out from behind a birch tree just ten yards away from us. Her white disc-like eye bulges out from under a mane of black hair that seems to have grown to her thighs overnight. Her complexion is as pale as the birch's papery white bark. What scares me most isn't the sight of her watching us—what scares me is that in the whole of three years this has been going on, she's never looked like that during the day.

And then a heavy pit opens in my stomach when I think about Mary and Michael and I grab Todd and rush him back toward the house. "Back to the house! Get back in the house! *Go!*" He falls when I shove him forward and I gather him up and set him on his feet and he runs to the house faster than I do. By the time I reach the edge of the backyard he's already ripping open the back door.

Idiot! Idiot! Idiot! Idiot! Idiot! Idiot! Idiot! *Idiot! Idiot! Idiot! Idiot!* That was what she was looking for! Making me think she never turned during the day, all this time just an elaborate fucking ruse to throw me off my guard and now Michael and Mary are—

I burst into the pool room and almost trip over the carpet in front of the chest freezer but I manage to grab the edge at the last second and steady myself before barrelling into the kitchen and sliding across the living room's pinewood floor. I almost slip again and nearly collide with Todd, who stumbles out of my way before I can fall against him.

Maureen, this one clothed casually with her hair done up in a bun, is sitting in her favourite chair in front of the fireplace while Michael and Mary sit on the couch comfortably and unharmed across from her, well out of her reach. She gives us a strange look, obviously alarmed by our dishevelled appearances and the fact that we're out of breath. "Hey, now. What are you guys up to?"

Relief washes over me. Relief and utter confusion. And then an abrupt surge of anger erupts within me. The lying bitch. The evil, lying bitch. "Maureen," I seethe, barely able to contain myself, "we need to talk."

The kids feel my rage emanating from me like heat wafting from a preheated oven that's just been opened. Their little eyes watch me tremble beyond my control as I stare daggers at their mother.

Maureen looks scared. In her short memory, this is a whole new side of me. Or maybe it *isn't* anything new to her, and hasn't been for a long time, and this is just an act. All one funny act. Slowly she rises from her chair and I grab her wrist and point my forefinger at the kids and utter one sharp command: "Stay here." And then I leave with Maureen in tow, complaining that I'm hurting her as I cross the kitchen and enter the foyer to lock the front door.

"Cameron! What's going on?" She's scared now, maybe for real—maybe *this* is an act, too. "Ow, Cameron—"

"Shut up," I snarl as I pull her through the house to the pool room. I lock the garage door and then swing her out onto the deck with such force that she fells against the floorboards and whines about scraping her knee. I turn and pull the door shut and lock it with the only key, which I conceal in my pockets. Then I turn on my heel and glower down at her as she sits up on her side, legs bent, knees hued red and oozing fresh blood from a few thin slits.

I know her disbelief is just a ruse. It has to be. "Cameron, *what* the hell are you doing?"

My eyes dart back and forth at the barren forest, at the trees protruding twistedly from a fiery orange surface that doesn't burn. I'm searching for the other Maureen, the wide-eyed witch hiding in the trees, as white as the snowy birches. A witch, a clever witch… a demon? A banshee? No, no… what *is* she?

"Cameron…?" She's caught on to my search and is now trying to dissuade me from my goal.

"Where is it?" I ask her.

"Where is *what*? You're not making any sense, Cameron! Christ, my knees…"

"You know goddamn well *what* I'm talking about, bitch! The chainsaw! Where. Is. *The chainsaw*?!"

"I don't know! I don't use it!" Her tone gets snarky as she rises to her feet: "Have you tried retracing your steps?"

I can see the thing within her twinkling in her eyes with its sly sense of humour and it takes everything I have not to pummel her right here and now. "Don't fuck with me. Don't fuck with me, Maureen. You don't want to fuck with me, Maureen. Because I'll kill you. I've done it before. I've done it a thousand times, and I'll kill you another thousand times, and another, and *another*—"

"Cameron, what the hell—?"

"Shut up! Stop pretending you don't remember! Stop acting like it only comes at night, because I just fucking *saw* you out there in the form you take when night falls! How stupid do you think I am, huh? How many more of you are out there? Which one of you took the chainsaw? Where's the fucking chainsaw?!"

"You know what? I don't have to listen to this shit. Fuck you. I'm going back inside." She moves for the door. I block her and she stops. "Move?"

"Like hell I'm letting you back in."

She makes another play for the door. Again, I stop her. "Get out of my way, Cameron."

"Where's the chainsaw?"

"I don't know, Cameron. It's wherever you left it. Jesus, move!" She tries to push me aside and I shove her back.

"Where's the chainsaw?"

"Cameron, you're drunk."

"I haven't had a drink all day," I say quietly. "Where's the chainsaw?"

"How many times do I have to say it?" she snaps. "I… did

not… touch… the *fucking* chainsaw! Why am I being blamed for this? You lose shit all the time."

"Like what?"

"Like… like the uh, the knive—cleaver! That went missing. Where's that, huh? We're stuck with an incomplete knife set, Cameron, because you lost the cleaver. I don't know *where* you lost it or *how* you managed to lose track of it, but you did.

"What about Buster, huh? He ran away because *you* weren't paying attention to how loose his collar was."

I'm shouting now, stabbing an index finger into her shoulder. "Don't you *fucking* talk to me like *I'm* the one who lost those things! *You* took the cleaver, just like you took the chainsaw! And Buster didn't run away, you—"

Shit…

Maureen glares at me expectantly, placing a hand on her hip. "I *what*? Huh? Go ahead—finish your sentence, Cameron. What did *I* do?"

I hesitate. The memory comes back, all too vividly. I remember being drawn to the deck by Buster's shrieking yelps. He made sounds that I'd never heard from him before, and never will again. The scarring image of her squatting on the near-black pool that flooded the patio, covered in blood and patches of strawberry-coloured fur. I remember seeing Buster's hindquarters on the edge of the patio separate from each other and the rest of him. The dog's steaming entrails were strewn across the snow that covered the yard at the time. I remember how clear the bright red saturation was in the snow under the patio light, back when we had one. She was tittering like a child with one of his paws in her cupped hands. The golden retriever's head was left at the bottom of the stairs, black marble eyes dulled after the life and joyfulness they once contained were ripped out of him. I never found his jaw and two thirds of his innards were gone forever, leaving only a hollow carcass for me to bury after the discovery.

Agitated by my silence, Maureen repeats her question, jolting me out of that horrific time, and I answer her with equal parts sorrow and anger: "You ate him."

She's taken back by this like she always is—or pretends to be. Which is it, exactly? "Excuse me?" she gasps. "I *what*?"

My voice shakes. "You *ate* my dog."

She doesn't seem to know how to react. Breaks into a nervous pace back and forth across the deck, fingers locked over her cranium, eyes shut, inhaling slowly, exhaling in a prolonged hiss, and after twenty seconds of this she stops in front of me again, eyes wide with anger and confusion. She shakes her rigid fingers in my face as she yells, "What drugs have you been taking, Cameron?"

"Drugs?"

"You're on something. What is it?"

"I'm not on anything."

"Yeah, I think you are. You know how I know that? Because it's making you crazy. *Look* at you! You're a strung-out mess. You're hurting me. You're threatening the kids. You told them I'm some kind of... of... demon or something? *Really*, Cameron? What's got you?" Her tone softens, though I still feel a soft edge hidden beneath it. "Cameron, you can talk to me, can't you? I can help you."

It won't work. It won't work. It won't work. I see right through your act. "Where's the chainsaw?" I ask again.

She sighs heavily with frustration and rolls her eyes. "Give it up, Cameron."

"You took the words right out of my mouth. Where is it? Where did you put it?"

"That's enough, Cameron."

I notice movement behind her and focus my attention on it and it's the *other* Maureen, the one with the distorted features despite the sun being up and she's staring at me and I'm staring back at her.

Maureen squints at me and turns around. She turns back and asks, "What're you looking at?"

My eyes flick to her. "You know damn well what."

"Cameron," she says slowly, cautiously, "you're really starting to scare me."

I grab her shoulders and shake her. I'm losing my patience with her. I'm really losing it. "You haven't *seen* scared yet, Maureen. *Where* did you put it?!"

"Let go of me!"

"I'm only gonna ask you one more time, Maureen."

"I don't know!" she shrieks, thrashing wildly. Her fingernails strike across my forehead and I know she drew blood because of how much it stings. I push her away and she manages to slap me before the momentum throws her out of reach. She steps back, a little too far, and her foot lands on the pool's tarp. She falls onto the tarp with a dull splash and the pool swallows her whole as the tarp folds in on her like jaws in a toothless mouth. Her mad thrashing is desperate, fearful, exacerbating her situation as she entangles herself underwater, the tarp's folds cocooning her.

It's a startling end to our fight. I watch paralyzed as the tarp's ends roll and twist in the water as a plastic vortex. Maureen's splashing subsides and the air bubbles stop fizzling on the surface and I know that she'd be dead by the time I got around to fishing her out.

The other Maureen witnesses this from her vantage point at the edge of the woods, maniacally warped features unchanged, owl-like eyes fixed on me in an unblinking, piercing stare.

I stare back at her, assuming a defiant expression. Anger flashes through me again and I scream at her. I scream and the wind carries it through the trees and a rush of birds take flight from their perches in them and fills the skies with their flapping wings. Orange torrents of fallen leaves spin and curl across the backyard in pursuit of the birds—nature's own autumn flashfire, erecting swirling pillars high in the sky. I scream until I'm red in the face and my vocals sting and tears well up in my eyes. By then the leaves have settled all over the pool and the deck, and the third Maureen I've encountered today is gone.

3:41 PM. In the pool room, I lock the door and then swing the screen back into place. I check the lock on the garage and find it's still pushed into the knob. Satisfied, I drag my feet to the kitchen and take a beer from the fridge, and then sit down in Maureen's chair by the kids. To my dismay, I realize they're watching *The Shining*, just as Jack Torrance starts to smash through the bathroom door with an axe to get to his shrieking wife on the other side.

"Jesus Christ. Christ," I mutter as I lurch for the remote on the coffee table. "This is a little intense for you guys." I change it amid a flurry of protests. "Be quiet. I'll find something more appropriate. Got to be something on here, it's a Saturday."

Todd pipes up: "Dad, it was getting good!"

"I don't care. Don't want you guys getting nightmares."

"Yeah, right," Michael sneers, pouting on his end of the couch. "Like we would ever get nightmares from the TV after the stuff that happens before bedtime."

The jab cuts deep, but I don't say anything to him about it, flicking through channels until I find some superhero cartoons for them to watch. "There." I drop the remote on the coffee table and return to the rocking chair, where I pull the tab off my can and guzzle it down. I look at the kids as they watch the TV, looking unsatisfied with my choice. "You don't like it you can switch to something else. But it's gotta be appropriate."

They don't bother moving. Mary asks me, "Where's mommy?" Her brothers turn their heads. Now all three of them are looking at me and a profound feeling of guilt presses down on my shoulders. I think for a time about how to answer them, though they damn well know what happened despite the earliness of their mother's murder.

"She's in the woods," I tell them, and add, "walking around somewhere." Technically I'm not lying to them—I always *hated* lying to them. They deserve to know the truth, but what good would the truth be for them?

"Why is she in the woods?" Mary asked.

I shrug. "I don't know," which is a lie, "she left without a word and she took the chainsaw with her," which isn't a lie.

Todd looks worried. He seems to be the only one of the three who's clued in to how frightening that thought is. Maureen is gone and so is the chainsaw. I'm scared too, Todd.

5:31 PM. I make spaghetti with ground beef and four cheese sauce for the kids. I don't make enough for myself. My appetite hasn't returned. My eyelids are heavy; my eyes burn. I empty my second beer and crush it against my skull, the bending tin crinkling loudly in my ears. The pressure gives me a headache and wakes me up. I toss the flattened tin chunk at the garbage next to the fridge and it flies wide, bouncing toward the front door instead.

Pull yourself together, goddamn it. You still have another twelve hours to go.

5:49 PM. Dinner is finally ready and I start taking platefuls of food into the dining room when suddenly I look out the picture window.

She's out there, bathed in the red glow of the setting sun, standing tall among the trees painted bloodily in the sunset's apocalyptic glare. She's watching me from the edge of the backyard and I know the kids will see her if we eat at the table tonight.

I take the plates into the living room and set them down on the coffee table. "Eat up."

They look at me, confused. Todd asks, "We're not eating at the table?"

I indicate the glass surface their plates are set on. "*This* is the table tonight." They give me weird looks, so I think up an explanation that should satisfy them: "It's Saturday, right? I figure we should have a movie night, just the three of us."

Mary asks, "Mommy's not back yet?"

"No," I say quickly. "She's busy still."

"When is she coming back?"

"I don't know. Eat up."

"What are we watching?" Todd asks.

"What do you want to watch?"

"A monster movie," Mary says.

"A grown-up movie," Todd says.

"I don't care," Michael says.

I grunt at their vague answers. "I'll see what I can find." I cross to the cabinet that stretches across the entire wall from the kitchen to the back of the living room and open one of its glass doors on the top shelf where a modest row of videotapes is stored. I run my finger along their cardboard sides, collecting a small layer of dust as I do so. My action and horror collection is mixed in with Maureen's period dramas and romantic comedies. Eventually my finger settles on *The Omega Man*, a tape I bought five years ago and never opened from its shrink-wrapping, and I take it over to the VCR on the top cabinet in the TV stand. I show them the cover. "How's this?"

They nod unanimously, though Michael doesn't seem too enthusiastic. And so, I put the movie in, and we watch Charlton Heston struggle to survive as the last man on earth.

6:24 PM. "Who wants popcorn?" The kids respond enthusiastically, so I get up and throw a bag in the microwave, and then dump the popped corn in a nice big bowl for the three of them to share. On my way back I pause in the doorway and peer across the dining room through the picture window and I see the bitch is still standing out there in her spot with her eyes never straying from the house, from *me*. Her eyes are eerie white dots in the dark blue hue of the coming night from where I'm standing.

Nervously, I pry my eyes away from her ghastly stare and enter the dark living room to give the kids their snack. And then I sit down in the rocking chair and look out the front window through the slits, gazing beyond the ramp at the front lawn and the trees that stand tall on the other side. I can still feel her eyes on me as if I'd never left the dining area.

6:59 PM. I notice something in the corner of my eye and I glance over at the kitchen entrance as something scuttles out of sight. A black blur. A *huge* blur. I get up and hurry toward the spot and search the kitchen. What the fuck was *that*? A rat? A *bigger* rat? Some other animal? I search the kitchen but I do not find it so I search the foyer next and then I look in the closet across from the basement door and then I throw open the basement door and look down the stairs into a dark, empty abyss. I shut the door and check the kids' rooms, but still I don't find anything out of the ordinary, so I check my room next, and then the bathroom, and now I'm frustrated because I *still* don't find anything. I know I saw *something*. I *know* it. What *was* it?

"Where the fuck are you?" I ask the thing I saw that might not exist. "Where could you be hiding?" I look behind the shower curtains and then I search all the rooms again, but I still don't find anything.

You're losing it, Cameron. You're really losing it. I snicker at my own paranoid delusions. Yeah, I must be.

7:13 PM. The movie's over. The kids undergo the process of preparing for bed while I return to my spot in the kitchen entrance in front of the picture window. She's *still* out there, watching us, watching *me*. I think about how she deceived me. Perhaps Maureen Morgan, the *real* Maureen Morgan, has been dead this whole time, ever since she was taken by her affliction. Maybe Maureen Morgan is nothing but a clever, cruel illusion created by this entity to trick us into thinking she was still with us, at least during the day. Maybe the Witching Hour was never real and just part of the entity's trap.

So why reveal itself now? I take a sip from my fourth can. Now *that's* something to be truly afraid of. What else has it led us to believe? Maybe it really *can* hurt me, and could have killed me whenever it wanted, and simply chose not to because I was the only one who had access to the children when it was strongest. But then, if the affliction isn't significantly weakened during the day, why couldn't it just do what it set out to do in the first place? Why go through the trouble?

To drive you mad, Cameron. That's why. This is not a being from a film or a book or a serial. This isn't the Amityville poltergeist or Michael Myers. It is pure, cruel, unrelenting, unhinged evil. This is an evil that *can* end it, that *could* have ended it any time it wanted to, but won't, because it *doesn't* want to end it; it *enjoys* it, and that is the coldest, hardest fact you will ever know. The fun ends when you end, Cameron. The children are simply the goal. You are the journey, and this bitch is taking every goddamn detour she, or *it*, can before it gets there.

"Dead end," I whisper, and then I chuckle at my stupid joke. I'm still staring at her. Goosebumps prickle on my arms and my senses are going wild with intense fear induced from her eyes alone.

So when Mary approaches me in the kitchen and tells me, "All done," I nearly jump out of my skin.

"Mary!" I gasp, pressing my back against the wall.

"Sorry," she says, looking genuinely ashamed. No, no, no, little dear.

I pick her up and hold her tight, carrying her through the kitchen before she gets a chance to look out the picture window, and I take her to bed, tuck her in under the covers. She looks concerned about something. "You okay, angel?"

"Mommy's still outside."

"Yes," I reply. "She's outside, but she's safe out there, just like you're safe in here." I grab her Raggedy Ann doll—one of the souvenirs left by the previous owners; Mary fell in love with it immediately—and nestle her beside Mary's head. "Ann will keep you safe."

She gives me an assured smile. Her face always glows when she smiles.

I smile back and kiss her forehead good night. "Sweet dreams."

"Good night, daddy."

I switch on the nightlight by the door and turn off the bedroom light, and the room goes dim. The window high above Mary's bed is an empty black square. I shut the door and lock it. Then I move on to the boys' room and I see them sitting up in their bunks reflected in the wall-to-wall sliding mirror doors. By the time I'm actually in the room, they're lying down, and I can't help but smirk at their vain attempt at sneakiness. "Settle down, boys. Lights out."

"Yes, dad," Michael responds.

"Okay, dad," Todd says. What a strange thing to hear from them. After months of silence, suddenly they're talking to me again. Weird. So weird.

A good weird.

"Shout if you need anything. I'm locking the door now." I wait a full five seconds before flicking their light off and shutting the door and snapping the lock into place.

7:37 PM. I do my best to repair the routine. It's all but shattered now, but if I'm careful it can be put back together. Even the most complex jigsaw puzzles can be whole again if you have all the pieces.

I make sure all the doors are locked, including the garage door, glancing instinctively at the beat-up car as I pass it, lamenting a time when I could actually drive it. I look down at the red blotch on the floor and stop to look at it. *Fresh* droplets? Maybe a few hours old? Well. Guess I should've waited until *after* I'd moved the dead Maureen from the trunk before scrubbing the floor. She must have been dripping while I was carrying her.

In the same spot?

Stranger things have happened.

I move on, check all the windows to make sure they're still secure, turning off the garage and the pool room lights as I head for the dining area. Maureen is still watching me from the woods. One glance is all I need to know she's still out there. I look through the other window behind my chair at the table, at the shed where now *another* Maureen stands statuesque, looking into the window at me. "Stop looking at me," I growl, "stop it. Stop it. Stop it." If only I had blinds. I leave the dining room and shut off the lights.

The basement's the last thing on my list. I head down there and search for anything out of place; any loose or broken windows, any disturbed knickknacks, fresh footprints, fingerprints, unsettled dust, the works. Nothing out of the ordinary.

I go around the bar and I'm met with the most horrific, ear-splitting screech I ever heard in my entire life and I nearly crash into a bookcase in my sudden fright. The rat I caught a glimpse of yesterday is now wriggling in full view on the glue trap. Its shrieking sounds almost human, a kind of suffering no one should hear from a living thing. I watch it squirm desperately, petrified by the suddenness of its shrill screams. This round, black mass of fur rocking back and forth, back and forth, trying to escape its snare, its fur detaching from its stuck limbs, revealing red glistening flesh beneath. The more it struggles, the more the glue latches on and peels off.

Utterly disturbed by its sounds, I turn and rummage through one of the lower storage cupboards and take out a bowling bowl and raise it above my head—just shut up shut up shut up shut up I'm sorry I'm sorry shut up—and with a loud, reverberating *thud* I drop the ball on top of the rat, silencing it for good.

8:29 PM. I'm sitting in the living room now with my sixth can of *Broweiser* beer. All the lights are off. The news on the TV is my only light source. I'm still shaken by the rat. The poor rat. What wrong did he do to deserve that? Why did I lay down such a cruel trap for such an innocent creature, repulsive though it may have been... it didn't deserve that, did it?

He's dead now. Let it go, Cameron. Let the poor little bastard rest in peace. You finished him quickly. That's about as humane as you can get. Clean it up tomorrow.

I watch the news anchor's mouth relay a pre-written script set on the table in front of him with glazed eyes. Heavy eyes. Eyes that burn. Eyelids... drooping... TV glare blinding now... shut my eyes just for a second... blink, damn you... just... blink... static ringing from the... TV... blink...

Part Four: Witching Hour, Sunday, October 22nd, 2000

Thunder claps and I jolt awake with a start and my eyes leap to the digital clock on top of the TV stand: 12:32 PM. No screaming. There's no screaming. Nothing but the wind howling and the rain's dull drumming against the windows and the roof. But she always screams. She *always* screams.

That's how I know something isn't right. She's not screaming.

The beer spilled while I was asleep and now there's a puddle on the floor next to the couch. I curse my clumsiness and set the can on a coaster on the coffee table and stand up. I rub sleep out of my eyes, blink a couple times, and then I conduct a cautionary patrol of the house. First thing I do is peek through the living room window overlooking the driveway and the front lawn. The rain comes down in a thick, soupy mist, masking most of the details in the view, reducing everything past the ramp into dark alien shapes. Lightning flickers briefly fill in the blanks with meticulous detail. I can make out Maureen's figure standing naked in the torrential downpour, seemingly erected in the middle of the driveway. Lightning again reveals how pale she is, darkening the shadows around her eyes before her features go black again. Another Maureen stands beside the birdbath. Yet another stands in the edge of my vantage point on the lawn facing the kids' windows. Good. She's out there. I'm in here.

Next thing I check is the dining room. I look through both windows and I don't see Maureen in either one. The chainsaw is missing and so is Maureen. I can feel cold, cold dread starting to claw its way up as I press on, entering the back and finding both doors still locked. Then I go through the kitchen and find the front door locked, too. The basement door is still closed. I tread quietly down the corridor toward my room—

—a whimper in the boys' room, almost too quiet for me to hear, but I heard. I heard, alright. My heart spikes. I press my ear against the door, hoping to hear something over the rapid pounding of my heart within my chest. My body breaks into a cold sweat and I can't stop myself from trembling. Stop shaking, damn you. Stop.

I have to know if they're alright.

Another whine, this one unmistakably real, and definitely Michael. I hear sobbing, too. It's faint, but noticeable. Todd, perhaps. Or maybe it's the other way around. Both of them are whimpering, one of them, or maybe *both* of them, are crying.

And then I hear someone shushing them, and Maureen's voice peels softly through the door like a breeze through an empty bottle: "Hush, children. Mommy's here."

My heart drops like a stone. No... she's *in* there *with them*! Quickly but carefully I fish my key out of my pocket and slip it into the body of the lock, and turn it, bracing my finger against it to keep it from snapping open and alerting her to my presence. The bitch, the bitch found a way in. The witch is in the room with my children. I slide the lock off and turn the door handle slower than I'd like to while the bitch continues to speak to them. "Michael, sweetie, you want that robot you saw in the ad, don't you? If you kill daddy for me, I'll buy it for you. I'll buy you all the robots you could ever want."

Todd stutters, "D-don't listen to her, Michael. No, don't..."

"Be quiet, Todd," Maureen admonishes him with a fierce hiss. "Mommy is speaking."

I open the door a crack and look in at the wall of mirrors and I see a black, slender thing that can't be human curving, *looming* over the bunk. My two boys cower under the sheets, unable to completely look away from the thing trying to coax them into doing her bidding.

I throw the door open and hit the light.

The thing standing between me and my children is *not* Maureen—it is an abstract bastardization of Maureen that shouldn't possibly exist. It stands above us all at about eight or nine feet, bending to keep from touching the ceiling. Its body is a collection of black rods, like strokes of India ink, with Maureen's head propped on its pencil-thin shoulders. Its head *swings* downward and dangles loosely, upside-down, and fixes its piercing glare on me and its body expands like the sail of a great medieval galley...

Maureen is shapeless and bow-like with giant fanning wings. Maureen is cunning. Maureen is blocking my view of my children from me.

I grab a wooden baseball bat leaning against the wall and I scream at the creature and swing the bat at it. Its wings disappear inside its stringy body and it recoils against the bunks and I hit it with the bat and it bends like rubber where I strike. It cowers, twining like a spring as I beat the bitch senseless with the bat, its arms depressing under the bat until I pound them into scribbly lines and they fall limp. Maureen's face lights up with terror and she screams again. I cock the bat and then bring it down on her skull, splitting it open, and I swing again, catching her ear. The wood vibrates sharply in my grip as the bat pulverizes the side of her skull, and everything inside that pretty head of hers explodes outward and splashes across the mirrors.

The boys lay still in their bunks, quivering like autumn leaves, crying. But they're alive. They're alive. Thank Christ they're—

The chainsaw squeals on the path outside and then I hear glass shatter and Mary screams behind the wall.

"MARY!" I bolt out of the boys' room and fumble for the key to Mary's lock. As I struggle to fit the key in, I yell at the boys: "Get out here! Get away from the windows!" The lock snaps open and I burst into Mary's room. Her bed's empty—no, God, *no*—the chainsaw, *my* chainsaw is bouncing frenetically in the window sill above her bed, its teeth spewing wood fibres. Mary screams again and I turn to see her curled up in the corner squeezing her Ann close to her chest and crying and shrieking in terror. "Mary!" I run in and pick her up and I hear Maureen howling over the chainsaw's deafening buzz. "You fucking bitch! You fucking bitch!"

I take Mary out of her room and I hastily throw the lock back on. Lot of good *that* will do now! Slow her down, gotta slow her down…

The boys are standing in the hall and Todd pulls their bedroom door shut and I throw the lock on that one, too.

Now what? Where do we go? What do we do now?!

"Dad!" Michael screams.

My mind races. I can barely hold Mary in my sweat-slicked arms. Bedroom can't stand against the chainsaw. It won't keep her back. Fuck, I… *fuck*! I knew it, I *knew* it, I—

Shut the fuck up, Cameron. Find a way. Find a way!

A loud crashing noise in Mary's bedroom throws the kids into a fearful frenzy. She's in the house. She's in the house and—

The chainsaw's droning gets louder behind the door and then the door shudders and the chainsaw's blade slices through the middle and starts running down, splitting the door in half, spraying sawdust into my back.

"Get to the garage!" I yell, shoving the boys down the hall. Only way. Gotta risk it. No other way. Oh, God, God, no.

The door splinters behind me and I turn and see Maureen with her tendrils twisted around the chainsaw's grips and her eyes penetrating the darkness like light reflecting off the flat of a knife's blade. "GIVE ME MY CHILDREN BACK!" She starts flailing the chainsaw across the walls, tearing the pictures down, slicing doorframes.

We're running in the dark with nothing but lightning showing us the way; the boys slide haphazardly across the kitchen's linoleum floor in their socks, little faces filled with an almost feral terror that I've never seen in them before. Mary keeps screaming in my arms as I run after them. "Don't look back, don't look back!" I tell them, but they don't hear me. Too scared for their lives to even notice the trio of Maureens slamming their palms on the picture window outside pressing their screaming, wide-eyed faces against the glass. They keep looking back; keep tripping over their feet, tumbling into the pool room.

Maureen whisks rapidly through the kitchen on her toes, chainsaw blade fragmenting dishes and flinging the toaster into the bottom of an overhead cupboard. She wails, "CAMERON! GIVE THEM BACK! GIVE THEM BAAAACK!"

I lock the entry to the pool room. I know the screen door won't hold. I look through the screen as she enters the dining area and stops, looking directly at me, tendrils wrapped tightly around the body of the chainsaw. More lightning blinks through the windows and Maureen's body glistens with a grotesque grey sheen. The harsh stormy winds batter the house until it shakes. Her feral eyes burn with white-hot rage. Tiny black pupils lock on to me and I shout, "Maureen, stop!"

She carries the chainsaw over to the dresser lining the wall opposite the picture window and runs the blade over our family pictures, blasting glass and little bits of metal and painted wood frames into the air as she cuts them down. Debris pelts the screen door. I hold Mary's face against my chest, keeping her eyes away from her demonic mother.

I back away and Maureen approaches the flimsy, transparent barrier between us. Her legs and arms begin to stretch, stilt-like, and two more spindly legs sprout from her middle. The boys throw open the garage door and yell at me for come with them, but I keep watching Maureen's transformation. The four-legged Maureen bends her legs in a crouch, and then her torso extends her head and her chainsaw-wielding hands toward the screen. One hand pulls on the door but it stays in place. With a frustrated yell, Maureen throws the chainsaw through the glass and slices up the screen mesh. Metal framework screams against the chainsaw's teeth and the grating screech startles me into action again and I leap into the garage and lock the door with Mary suffocating in my constricting arms.

"Daddy," she whines, "I can't breathe! I can't breathe!"

I'm quick to slacken my hold around her. "I'm sorry, honey. I'm sorry." My mind races as I scan the garage for anything to use against the chainsaw. The boys run to the shutters and try to lift them. I yell, "No! No! No! No! No! Leave it alone! Get away from there! Get away! You'll let her in!"

The chainsaw squeals behind the door and then the blade penetrates through its solid oak mass and the kids scream again. I set Mary down on the dark spot next to my car and grasp the bars on a utility shelf in front of the car, and pull it on its side over the stairs as a crude blockade. Tools and canisters and scrap crashes deafeningly to the floor. I squint against the cloud of sawdust spraying out of the door, careful to keep my fingers away from the chainsaw as it thrusts through the door again and starts carving a wicked slant down the middle. I wedge the top of the shelf in a niche between the doorframe and a support beam and pray that it'll hold long enough for me to get the car prepped. Gotta risk it. Gotta risk it. No choice. No other way. Flies in a spider's web.

I go round the car and climb up the shelf bolted into the wall until I reach a safe box up top. I turn the dial: 9-13-24; the days each child was born in order. It clicks open and I take out the jerry can, the last bit of precious fuel in this house, and the only gun that still has bullets in it, a .38 snub nose revolver (which I promptly stuff into my back pocket), and I jump down to the floor—

Mary screams and then the boys scream and I whirl around to see Mary *ascending* toward the ceiling and my eyes focus on two long black arms reeling her up into a hatch in the ceiling.

A hatch… *the attic*! The jerry can slips through my fingers.

"Mary!" I'm already grabbing a flashlight and tearing a ladder off the wall, watching my little girl kick her legs as the inhuman limbs bring her level with the fluorescent light tubes in the rafters, one of which she shatters in her vain struggles to get free. The boys and I leap out of the way of falling glass and sparks. The chainsaw connects with the shelf and its teeth grind against the shelf's metal posts.

Not my baby not my baby not my baby not my—

The top of the ladder barely has time to hit the wall before I start scaling the fucking thing like a rocket lifting off into space. Mary disappears in the hatch and her screaming little voice can still be heard in the attic, fading as it crosses toward the far wall, soon to be above the living room.

"Mary! Mary!" I scramble up the ladder and reach the open hatch.

The boys scream, "Dad!" and I look down at them and they're pointing at the door, so I look at the door and I see a piece of solid oak fly out of the door.

Maureen gets to work on another section in the door but I still have time so I flick the flashlight on and assure my sons, "I'll be back down before she can get through! Michael, get in the car! Todd, gas it up! Jerry's can over there! *Hurry*!" They do as they're told. Good boys, good boys.

Mary's screaming rises in pitch and I can hear her again. I suck in air and leap through the hatch and shine the flashlight on—

A fucking *horde* of Maureens, all distorted and gruesomely misshapen, missing one or two limbs each. A hundred eyes gaze angrily at me from every corner in the low-ceilinged attic. I run the flashlight's beam across the throng and my heart crystalizes into solid ice and I damn-near slip and fall down the ladder from the shock of seeing Maureen, so many Maureens, all of them having hidden themselves away in this fucking attic all this time! They were above us. All this time they dwelled in secret and I never fucking *thought* of the possibility that so many of them could have been up here without my noticing. I look down at the floor and it's caked in a thick, slimy layer of gore and then I notice the putrid smell of rotting death and mould. The dust stings my eyes but I'm too horrified to blink, too startled by this new revelation to look away from all these squatters, and I notice a hand moving on its own accord until I shed light on it and realize it's dragging a fully emotive head behind its wrist.

Mary's shrill begging for me to save her kicks my reflexes into overdrive. I throw myself onto the floor and I scream at the cowering things in my way, using my light source as a weapon to drive them away. The light keeps them at bay and forces them to scuttle out of its glare. "Get the fuck away! Get away! GET AWAY!" One of them lurches her one-eyed face mere inches from mine and hisses. I drive my fist into her face and dig my thumb into her one good eye and push it in, eliciting a pained howl from its lungs. "Mary!"

"DADDY!" I swing the flashlight in the direction of her voice and the Maureens scatter like fearful mice, revealing to me a trio of them holding Mary down on a dusty old box while a fourth raises a blood-darkened cleaver that gleams viciously in the light. "Daddy!"

"Mary!" I yell. I feel tendrils snap at my heels. The bitch's face rears its deformed head out from behind me and sinks its teeth in my arm and I feel burning pain shoot up into my brain but I don't stop because I'm too focused on the knife and I tear my arm out of the thing's mouth and then—

And then the cleaver comes down and its dull edge sinks into Mary's right shoulder. My little girl, no, no, they're butchering my little girl! She screeches and wriggles erratically but those three fucking bitches keep her down on the box. The cleaver comes up once more and I roar, "STOP IT!" I direct the flashlight at the butcher and it lurches away with a high-pitched wheeze and I'm almost there, I'm almost there, baby—I shine the flashlight at the trio and they yelp like dogs being kicked but one of them grabs Mary's loosened arm and tears it out of its socket and Mary's wailing only gets louder. "MARY! MARY!"

I reach her and I see blood spurting out of the stump in my little girl's shoulder and a new wave of horror and fury explodes from within. I grab her other hand and overpower her flailing and yell over her screams, "Mary, Mary, it's okay! It's okay! Put pressure on it! Press your hand over it! Mary!" Her crying understandably continues; she's frantic, screaming for me, telling me it hurts, but she keeps her hand where it hurts nonetheless, her blood spilling through her short, thin fingers.

The butcher snarls, blurring in the darkness with her cleaver raised for another strike. I blind her with the flashlight and kick her kneecap back and duck out of the way as it crashes to the floor. Then I wrest the cleaver out of her fingers and I turn the thing on her body and her skull and I don't stop butchering the butcher until the group of squatters begins to swell in on us and I turn the cleaver on them in a blind rage, swinging in the dark, slicing off limbs, splitting faces, cleaving skulls and sending heads flying through the air but still they persist, clumsily avoiding the beam of light in my hand and trying to get behind me. I feel their claws rake across my back and their jagged teeth nipping at my joints and I feel pain all over. I don't stop until I see the one that has Mary's arm and I see the bitch indulging herself in Mary's severed flesh, and the blood spurting out when she bites down attracts the others and they trample and fight each other for their own piece of Mary's arm. I kill one that lingers behind by dropping the blade in her chest and I look the evil bitch in the eye and I tell her, "Found the cleaver, Maureen! I found it! I found the cleaver!" I rip it out of her and she collapses.

Mary's screaming fades to agonizing moans that peel through the attic, almost overpowering the roar of the chainsaw and Todd's desperate cries for my return down below because the witch is almost in the garage.

I run back to Mary and see one of her restrainers on all fours over Mary's blood that has dribbled down the side of the box and gathered into a puddle, lapping it up off the floor like a dog. I bring the cleaver down on the back of her head, nailing her face to the floor before taking it back out and shining the flashlight on Mary's other restrainer. I pursue it as it darts toward a nearby corner— except it doesn't get that far because I manage to grab it by the ankles, drag it back and separate her face into mushy little sections while screaming, "Found it! Found it! Found it! Found the cleaver! I found it! It's right *here*, Maureen, right here, can you see it, can you *feel* it?!"

The others are done with Mary's arm and hungry for more. My flashlight disperses them into the far side of the attic, their shrill taunts and screams hurting my ears. I pick up Mary and run back toward the hatch post-haste because unless I do something my daughter will die and the other Maureen will have breached the oak door. I bite down on the cleaver's blade and keep my tongue tucked in the back of my mouth to avoid tasting the months and months' worth of dried blood on it.

The others are converging on us now, squealing profanities and threats and demands now that they know they will never taste Mary again if I can help it. I hold her against me and I step down on the ladder and start a quick descent, assaulting the squatters with one last sweep of light before leaving it on the floor, facing them.

My legs are almost mechanical the way they scale down the rungs and I pause only for a second to see that half the oak door is gone and Maureen is in the process of climbing over the shelf. I clear the rest of the ladder and throw the driver's side door open and drop the cleaver on the seat so that I can carefully set Mary down in the passenger seat. The boys gasp in horror and ask me what happened to her, if she's alright, if she's dead, "Is my sister dead?!"

"Where's her arm? What happened?!"

I yell, "Is it gassed?" and Todd nods quickly before asking me the same question about Mary again. "Give me the blanket behind you." Michael stands on his knees and pulls the folded blanket under the rear window down. I glance over at the door and Maureen feet have just landed on the floor. "Hurry! Hurry up! Fuck!"

Maureen pounces with the chainsaw. I scream and duck behind the door and hear the chainsaw's teeth scrape the top and the chainsaw gets deflected. Five of the entities stick their faces through the hatch as jeering spectators expecting my long-awaited execution.

I throw myself behind the wheel and pop the cigarette lighter out. ""Press the blanket—"

The chainsaw bursts through the door window and shreds the flesh above my right elbow, spattering my blood on the back seat window, making Michael break into fearful tears. "Dad!"

I gnash my teeth. Fight the pain, fight the pain, fight the pain. I look at Mary, her skin pale, her wound oozing onto the seat. "Press the blanket on her stump. S-stop the bleeding!"

Maureen laughs triumphantly. It's something out of my worst nightmares, like a beat's bellowing laughter echoing through the caverns of hell. She cocks the chainsaw back, her foot slamming the door against my legs, trying to pin me against the seat.

The chainsaw comes down. I kick against the floor while shoving the door outwards and lurch back with the cleaver just as the chainsaw roars through the window and guts the driver's seat, filling the interior with stuffing. The boys scream in terror. I pat Michael's window to assure them I'm still alive but my eyes are entirely focused on the bitch lifting her chainsaw out of the car. Her piercing stare lets up only for a moment to glance at the boys in the back seat with a hungry longing. Predatory eyes watch Michael press the bunched-up blanket against his sister's bleeding socket.

The sight only fuels my anger. I raise the cleaver. "Get the fuck away from my kids, you evil fucking *CUNT*!"

Maureen's face twists in my direction again, distorting further with hate and disgust, eyes growing even wider. Her mouth a narrow slit that releases a gurgling hiss. She advances. I take a step back toward the shutter door. Glass from the broken light tube crunches under her bare feet, making her cringe. She doesn't falter. Chainsaw pointed at me. I keep my distance. All I've got's a fucking cleaver. Jesus, Jesus, Jesus, God, she's gonna kill me in front of the kids. She's gonna kill them next and the last thing they'll see is their father lying on the floor in pieces—

Stop it, stop it, stop thinking like that. Focus. Focus! Avoid the chainsaw. Follow the chainsaw. She hasn't killed you yet. That's not about to change.

Maureen attacks the window the boys are behind instead! Shatters it and shoves the blade inside and I see their heads fly to the other side of the back seat and blood splash across the rear window and I fucking *lose it* I charge at her and she suddenly turns and I feel the blade rip into my side and skin my elbow. A goddamn clever trap, I'll give her that one—and it almost worked. I yell in agony, throwing myself against her, grabbing hold of the chainsaw's handle with my right hand and swinging the cleaver into her eyes with my left. She rears her head back for a deafening cry of sheer anguish, cleaver still embedded in her face, and then I rip the fucking chainsaw out of her tendrils and I drive the blade into her stomach and she screams even louder, tendrils once again wrapping themselves around its body and squeezing my arm. I relish every fucking second I have to make this one suffer and I pull the chainsaw up and split her ribcage wide open, spilling her innards on the floor, jets of her blood spraying the wall behind her and the side of the car. Then I jerk it up through her neck and her head swings lopsidedly over her shoulder as both sides of her upper torso bend in opposite directions.

She crumples against the wall, much to the dismay of the squatters. I turn off the chainsaw and toss it, noticing right away that the squatters have fallen silent, simmering up there in the ceiling, unwilling to come down just yet. I look up at them, and glance at the car to see my boys alive, though Michael has a bloody gash in his shoulder where the chainsaw got him. It's bleeding badly. I look at Mary and she's asleep. That's all. Just sleeping. Has to be sleeping. Can't be dead. Can't be.

I kick the ladder off the wall and it clatters against the shelf barricade, and then I climb into the car, lift the key out from under the seat, start it up, and then shut my door, stealing one last upward glance as I do so. "Seatbelts," I breathe. "Seatbelts, put them on, brace yourselves, okay? Stay with me, Mary. Don't leave me. You can't leave me. I'm gonna take you to the hospital, okay?" I shift into reverse and floor it. The car lurches back and slams into the shutters and the shudders bend outward, sounding a lot like the thunder outside. I shift into drive and push the gas down hard enough for the car to jolt forward and bump into the overturned shelf.

Maureen plummets from the hatch and lands on all fours. "Cameron!"

Once again, I shift into reverse and floor it. The car bursts through the shudders, taking one of the flexible strips of metal with us as it wraps around the back end of the car. I swerve across the driveway and slew sideways, flinging the strip away. The car stops only a moment, as it now faces the end of the driveway. Drive. I throttle it and the car shoots down the driveway with four more of these bitches screaming frantically and giving chase. The car drops down, skids to the bottom of the rain-slicked slope and I almost end up in the ditch right there. I jerk the wheel and the wooden mailbox with THE MORGANS painted in big white letters is blown to splinters and scattered across the hood and over the roof.

We're on the road now and the rain is still pouring down and it's all downhill from here—literally. A sidewinder down the side of what may as well be considered a mountain bristling with birches, veined by a single road that loops around on itself, dotted by no more than five houses.

I know the neighbours will be useless. The neighbours won't understand. They'll die by Maureen's hands. And if they don't? If they're competent? If they're medical experts whose speciality just happens to be saving patients with lost limbs, or if they actually have the mental capacity to call an ambulance? My brain keeps telling me to stop at one of the houses. Stop at one of the houses, Cameron, do it. But what if they're not home? What if I crash the car when I make an attempt to stop? I'm driving without goddamn brakes.

Hospital's just ten kilometres from here. *Just... ten... kilometres.* If I'm gonna crash the car to stop it anyway I should do it in a sure place. "Hold on, Mary! Hold on! Michael, keep that blanket on her! Keep it on her!"

SHE WATCHES ME BURY HER

*

3:46 AM. Thunder claps and I bolt upright in my seat. A sudden jolt of hot pain slithers up into my cranium and stays there. Vision blurred. Can't tell which way is up. Rain's still coming down hard, pitter-pattering heavily on the ceiling. Pounding in my ears. I deflate the airbag and squint through a windshield that doesn't exist anymore. Thoughts returning. No amount of fog in my brain can make me forget—

"Mary!" I turn slowly and see my little girl sprawled in her seat, pressed into it by the airbag, skin as white as porcelain, pajamas drenched and saturated with her blood. I quickly deflate the airbag and feel her neck for a pulse. No... she's cold. Mary... Mary! "MARY!" I turn her face toward me and she still looks peaceful, like she's sleeping. But I know she *isn't* sleeping my little angel is *dead*, she's *dead* and that bitch Maureen her mother *killed* her. I fall over and wrap my arms around my baby and sob into her shoulder. I can feel my heart falling to pieces that seem to only get heavier the more they crumble into sharp little pieces of shrapnel that stab the inside of my chest. Little sowing pins, a whole ruptured bag of them piercing me from within, unrelentingly painful, and my tears blind me as I hold her close to me. Can't stop shaking. Can't stop shaking.

Until something *jolts*: a sudden realization that I'm alone in this car because my boys haven't said anything, and then trepidation spikes, hard and heavy, as I look into the back and find it empty and my broken heart flares. No, not *them*, too. Michael, Todd, please, *please* let *someone* be alive!

My .38 is still in my back pocket. I take it out and check the cylinder. All six chambers are loaded. Six shots. I snap it shut and keep my forefinger on the trigger guard—*always* on it... unless the bitch is spotted. Last thing I want to do is shoot my own kids.

Handle doesn't work. It takes three kicks to get the door open. I step out and slip on wet grass and splash in muddy puddles, I look at the tree that is now leaning away from me; the hood of my car is wrapped around its base and it comes back.

We never make it. I hit a turn too hard, so focused on getting Mary to a doctor. Roads too slippery. Tires didn't catch. Slid right off the road like it was magically lifted up by a giant hand and turned on its side—right into a tree. My boys. Where are my boys? One of the back doors hangs open. The other one is jutting up out of a ditch. No rear window.

Hit my head. Can't see properly. Rain making it all a haze. Lightning blinds me. Can't make out a goddamn thing until I turn around and see a quartet of orange orbs glowing in the black storm. Kids must be there. Boys must've seen the light. My Mary…

My eyes burn as fresh tears blend with the rain hitting my face and I almost collapse as the realness of Mary's death sinks its claws into me and digs its way in. My eyes are burning and my stomach feels like it's shrivelling in a different kind of fire.

My boys… have to find my boys… go to the lights. They must've gone to the lights. Maybe they provided them small comforts in this blackness. Can't even see the road.

The orange glare quickly becomes four upward cones shining on a wrought-iron gate that reads ST. BERNARD'S CEMETERY. The cemetery. The fucking *cemetery*. I got distracted by what Henry had told me: that he found Maureen out by the cemetery. Distracted, right before that turn came up and I killed Mary…

Stop. Stop. Stop. Find Michael. Find Todd. They're out here somewhere. "Boys!" I shout, passing through the gate. Thunder rumbles above me. "Todd! Michael!" Please, God. "Todd! Michael!" Please, God, please, please, please. Lightning fills the cemetery with stark white, showing me the main road that cuts through endless rows of gravestones of varying size, lined with leafless, towering oaks.

I was stupid to leave the flashlight at home. Now I'm wandering through the cemetery with a concussion and two missing children. "Michael! Todd!" I squint through the sleet and press on, looking to my left and waiting for lightning to show me the empty rows of graves. Look to my right and wait for another rod to illuminate the tombstones embellished with withering flowers. No kids. The wind carries a low-pitched moan to my ears and my heartrate spikes because I know that sound well enough to know that even *if* my boys aren't here, I'm still not alone.

The witch followed us. She's looking for them. The bitch, *she* killed my Mary.

Yes, Cameron. Yes. *She* killed Mary. And if you don't find them soon, she'll kill Michael and Todd, too. Snap out of it, Cameron. You can't break down now. Not *now*!

Maureen's cries sound almost mournful as they echo through the cemetery, distorted by the gusts of storm winds rushing across the sloppy wet ground. I break into a mad dash into oblivion. I don't know where I'm going or what I would or *could* do if I found the boys or if I ran into *her* instead.

I run with clumsy abandon down the muddy path, kicking up clumps of grass, feeling the mud trying to suck my feet into them, soaking through my socks.

Feet.

I stop and look down and wait for lightning to strike again, and when it does I take advantage of its strobe-like flicker to search the drenched earth for a sign. Nothing the first time. I stand completely still, keeping my eyes on the spot I was looking before the light faded, and then more lightning, and I search again and through the heavy rain find two sets of flooded footprints behind me, trailing back towards where I just came from. I follow the tracks, keeping my eyes on the ground where I saw them, though I can't see them now. I wait for another flash before I see where they actually go, and I track them toward the grass, pass an oak tree and down an aisle of crosses. Nothing *but* crosses up here, all lined up neatly in seven rows down an incline that proves to be a challenge in this relentless storm with a wounded dog howling at my back in the distance.

That's not a dog. Don't kid yourself, Cameron. She's closer, getting so much closer…

The mud catches harder than I anticipate and brings me down and a startled shout escapes my lungs as I fall on my free hand and knees with a splash.

As if I'm not already drenched, anyway.

I look up at a cross and pull myself off the ground with it. Then I look down and search the ground again, waiting for lightning to guide my eyes to my boys' footprints. It's delayed, and it makes me worry. Another hysterical cry echoes in the distance, closer than before. God, please, hurry up…

Lightning! Their paths curve off the aisle and start cutting between gravestones a few paces behind me. Almost missed them. I rush between three sets of marble crosses in pursuit and instinctively glance to my left, back toward the main road, and another lightning strobe reveals *dozens* of misshapen Maureen variants all crossing the main road.

Jesus Christ, the place is *teeming* with them—and I'm leading her *right* to them!

No. I can't do that. I *won't*.

Lightning. I see that the boys' trail dots the side of the hill, continuing behind the crest into a small valley full of small mausoleums. I can see the wrought-iron fence surrounding them from where I'm standing and quickly deduce that they ran in that direction into the woods far beyond the cemetery's borders, or hid in the mortuary just outside the woods, *or* they're hiding in one of the mausoleums.

Goddamn it, which one?!

Maureen's off-key choir makes the most horrible, grating noises as they swarm the cemetery, flowing in the direction that the boys' tracks go. She doesn't even need to *see* their footprints to know that the track goes to the mausoleums. It's as if she's *drawn* to them. It wouldn't have mattered if I fired a shot in the air and ran in the opposite direction—it's not *me* she wants.

I bolt over the hill, gunning for the mausoleums, feet pumping through muddy patches that cling to my feet and pull my socks off, trying to slow me down. I can't slow down. I *can't*.

I reach the top of the next incline when my big toe slams into the side of a small gravestone protruding from the ground. I feel my toenail snap off and the bone splitting in my flesh and the pain shoots up my leg so fast that I barely have time to register that my desperate run has dissolved into a tumble down the slope and I'm smothered by soaked grass and slippery mud while the hard edges of tombstones slash my arms and pierce my sides. The world spins around me like a kaleidoscope filled with black and grey patterns in varying shades. Feels like my brain is getting scrambled inside my aching skull. Then my tumble abruptly ends with my back smashing a flowerpot into the base of a tombstone. My head's still twisting and turning. Vision going blank, blurred by the rain. Feel myself passing out...

But I *don't* pass out. Don't pass out, Cameron. Get up. Hear that? Do you hear her? She's close now, Cameron, closer than ever, so get up, *get up*!

And I do, sensitive to every little shock of pain blazing in my broken toe. I don't dare look at the injury and limp as quickly as I can to the gate that locks them in, and I wonder how the fuck they can possibly be *in* there if there's a chain and lock keeping the gate shut. I look in through the bars at the mausoleum rows and the lightning flickers, revealing to me a name scrawled on the mausoleum that sits opposite the gate, at the very end of the row, hazy in the rainy sleet, but I can just make it out: THORN. I have no time to think about the significance of this because the first of the Maureens have reached the path only two hundred paces behind me, and I wrack my brain for where, just *where* the boys could possibly be—

The mortuary! They *have* to be there!

I stagger to the corner of the fenced valley and look out just as more lightning flashes its stark whiteness on the cemetery, revealing further rows of modest headstones and the mortuary with its rear facing the forest, and I start hobbling as fast I can toward it, glancing back to see all those Maureens. They're a wide-spanning, shapeless mass of gruesome shapes and wild eyes scuttling after me like frightened rats. They're no longer screaming or snarling or shouting at me. They are silent wraiths in the dark whose footfalls don't seem to be registered by my own ears or the earth itself. It's like they're not even there—but they *are* there, *right* there, following me post-haste, and so I race awkwardly for the mortuary, praying that my boys are there, that they'll be safe in there even with her outside.

Three more rows and I glance over my shoulder at the mass as it spreads across the graveyard like a black wildfire, spilling around tombstones as well as creeping over them, their eyes fixed unblinkingly on me. Mud continues to hinder my progress. My toe burns excruciatingly and my head pulsates with numbing pain with every step I take. Press on, I press on, pushing past tombstones as I limp ahead of Maureen to the mortuary door. The gap between me and that goddamn door isn't closing nearly as fast enough as the gap between my back and my wife is. "Todd!" I scream. "Michael!" I keep limping through the mud, stumbling in the rain. I'm close enough now that I can see the door clearly. I look back again and I see that one of them is almost within striking distance, reaching for my injured foot. I draw my .38 in the demonic thing's direction and blast its eye through the back of its head and it slumps dead over a headstone. "Boys! Open up! Boys!"

What if they're *not* in the mortuary? Oh, Jesus, what if I'm wrong and they're in the woods instead?

The mortuary door flies inward and two frightened little faces peek out of the darkness at me and the relief of seeing them both alive with the combination of Maureen's sudden shrill wailing peeling out from behind me makes me limp even faster. Almost there, not much farther! Run, goddamn it! *RUN*! The boys shout encouragements at me, tinged with fear that I won't make it and the determination that I will, both fighting each other for supremacy in their voices. I'm coming, boys, I'm almost there, almost—

"Behind you!" Michael screams, and I whirl to face another Maureen as she springs off a headstone, claws forward, her mouth stretched wide and unleashing a terrible screech as she descends upon me.

I fall against a cross and my .38 barks and she chokes on the bullet in midair and I leap away and she slams into the cross, knocking it over.

God, they're *everywhere*! Closing in. Dozens, *hundreds* of them are all around us screaming their terrible chorus that rips into our ears and makes us wince. They're almost at the door—so am I.

I dive in between the boys and they yell fearfully as they shove the door back into place—

"Children, my children!"

—not all the way. The door slams into her arm, nearly severing it. The boys don't stop pushing, pressing their full weight against the door as the horde outside batters it with their fists and the one arm locked in the space lashes out, claws scraping the door above Michael's head.

"Dad!" Todd yells.

Michael whimpers, clamping his eyes shut as the door shudders against his uninjured shoulder.

I'm on my feet in two seconds, further hindered by my broken toe. I limp to the door, dodging a couple thrashes from Maureen's arm before snatching her forearm and pushing it back outside, but her elbow's still caught in the door, and now hundreds of fingers are latching themselves around the edges of the door and the boys' attempt to keep them back starts to wane in Maureen's favour. I peer into the narrow strip between the door and the frame at the distorted face that belongs to the elbow, and my .38 burns a tunnel through that face. The body reels back and takes its elbow with it.

"Push *NOW*!" I roar, and in a final surge of strength the boys slam the door into place, severing the fingers which then fall to the floor like droppings, resulting in another series of agonized moans from outside. I flip the lock and pull the boys away from the gathering of fingers that writhe and quiver on the floor. Once we're a safe distance from the door I can't stop myself any longer, and I fall to my knees and embrace them both tight against me and the tears can back, tears of relief and emotional agony. "I'm sorry. I'm so sorry. I'm sorry, boys. I'm sorry. Thank God, thank God you're okay. You're both okay." I peck their heads and faces with kisses until they tell me to stop, and I do, but I can't stop sobbing even after we've separated.

"Dad...?" Michael says, near tears himself. "Where's Mary?"

Todd stares at me with wide eyes, *pained* eyes, and I know he already knows what happened to Mary.

"She's gone." I can barely get the words out of my mouth, and when I do, the pins in my chest and stomach start piercing me from within again and they don't stop. "God, I... she's gone." I fall against the wall and slide to the floor.

Todd breaks into tears. Michael does, too, but to a lesser extent—still confused, still trying to realize how real it is, how to really hear it: "What do you mean she's gone, dad? What do you mean she's gone?"

"Mary's dead, Michael." Todd falls against me and hugs me and wails into my shoulder and I hold him tight and stroke his head. "She's dead, she's... she's gone." My voice is broken between sobs. Can hardly breathe. "She's gone."

Michael starts to shake. His face contorts, devastated, and he collapses on his knees and sniffles. The tears don't stop flowing down his cheeks.

I hold my hand out to him. "Come here. It's okay, Michael. It's okay. Come here."

He crawls over to me and buries his face in my chest and lets it all out. "It's okay," I assure him, voice cracking.

There are only two windows in the mortuary, both facing east on either side of a clock. Glass and limbs explode out of them and Maureen's shrieks fill the empty room. Pieces of glass skitter across the unoccupied steel table sitting next to the incinerator.

"It's okay," I tell them, holding their heads against me, my .38 resting on the floor beside me. I feel their bodies trembling violently on my outstretched legs.

The door takes another hit. The top hinge pops out and a bolt tinkles on the floor. The lock strains against the impacts. Won't be long now before they're inside. Like hell I'm letting her take them from me, too.

"Shhh," I whisper to them as a strange calm washes over me. This is it. The end. I don't have enough bullets to kill all the

Maureens. I can't protect them that way.

But I *will* protect them. I'll do whatever it takes to keep her away from them.

My hand slides away from Todd's air. My mud-caked fingers twist around the grip of the .38 and lift it up.

The door takes another hit. Sounds like a freight train ramming into a truck. The whole building shakes.

"I'll protect you. I promise."

Two Maureens start clambering through the window. Fingernails scrape the table's surface. Won't have to look at those piercing eyes in just a minute.

I take a deep breath, hold it for a moment, and then my breath shudders upon releasing it. "I love you, boys. I love you more than anything in the world."

The door blows open and *they* come scrambling in. I feel my children tense up.

I brush the muzzle of the .38 against Todd's head, and before he can react to it I shoot him. Michael leaps at the sound and looks at me, but I don't give the poor child enough time to register what I've done to his brother until I quickly do the same to him and they both fall against me again and I feel their warm blood soak through my shirt.

The Maureen-things stopped dead when the first shot rang out. Now they are standing there, looming above me, staring at me and the dead children I've got huddled in my arms. They start twitching furiously, without a word or a sound coming out of their mouths. Convulsing, then *crumbling* to the floor, first in grieving positions on their knees, heads lowered, faces distended in anguish, mouths agape in silent screams of agony—and then *dust* as grey as ash.

All but one of them. The last Maureen's grotesque features fade back into the beautiful, human woman I originally married. The woman I fell head-over-heels in love with so many years ago back in college. The first time I saw her, I knew she was the woman I was going to marry. She was intelligent. She was objective. She was even brave when she needed to be. She was unwavering. She was once a gentle soul that bent to no one's will. Incorruptible, or so I thought, before we moved into that house. Before *this* happened.

I glance at the clock: 4:27 PM. The affliction is gone. All it took were the deaths of our three children.

And now, when I look at her *now*, I see nothing but the catalyst for the end of my life. When I look at her pitiful form; as I watch her cry hysterically at the sight of Todd and Michael, the states I put them in to protect them from her, I see nothing but a vessel taken by an entity whose evil is as unstoppable as its vessel's resolve, and as intelligent as she is. I see a dangerous combination that is now missing a vital component.

I see a wounded mother who has just snapped out of her mania and realized that in her possessed lunacy, she killed her three children.

"Maureen," I say to her, and she doesn't react to my voice right away, sobbing uncontrollably instead. "Maureen," I call out, and this time she *does* look up, teary eyes already glazed over, her face apparently aged twenty years in such a short time.

"Cameron?" She sounds confused.

"I love you," I assure her, "I love you so much. You have no idea. I saved them *from* you... I saved them *for* you."

And then I shoot her in the head. She flies back, sprawled out on the floor in the far corner of the mortuary.

I look down at the boys. They look so peaceful. They're so... warm. I stroke their heads and I plant a kiss on each of them before I raise my chin up and point the muzzle of my .38 upwards against the soft tissue under my mouth, and I close my eyes. Finally, we'll be together again, far away from here.

I pull the trigger.

The hammer smacks into an empty chamber. No... can't be. I try again. Click. Please.

Click.

God, please.

Click.

Please!

Click.

Click.

No! No! *No*!

Click.

Click.

Click.

No...

Part Five: Sunday, October 22nd, 2000

7:05 AM. It takes a while for me to get up, but eventually I do, and the first thing I do is leave the mortuary, cross the graveyard back to my car, back to Mary. I take Mary out and I carry her back to the mortuary, and part of me is astonished that no one, not even the church-going folk, notices my activities or the car wreck in the ditch.

Back in the mortuary, I lift my dead wife off the floor and position her in the incinerator, and then I place the children around her, barely managing to fit all four of them inside. I set the gun down at their feet. Then I shut the door and ignite the flames and let it go as hot as it'll go. For a time, I stand in front of it, watching them burn peacefully, the flames consuming them, taking them to a place far away from this cruel world.

"Ashes to ashes," I whisper, "dust to dust." I do not cry. I do not feel anything. Emptiness, perhaps. A strange tingling grief in the back of my skull. But I do not cry. Not anymore, now that they are at peace, reunited with their mother.

8:45 AM is when I finally leave and start the long trek back up the hill toward the house. Halfway there, a young gentleman in a pickup truck notices me limping barefoot along the road and asks me where I'm going.

I guess he can't see the blood in my shirt. Helps that I'm wearing black. "Up that hill," I tell him, pointing at the mountain bristling with orange leaves and white birch trees and brown oaks and maples. It's a big, beautiful mound jutting up toward a clear blue sky.

"Sure, I can take you there. Hop in."

I thank him and climb into the passenger seat.

"How far up?"

"When you see a driveway without a mailbox."

He's a bit confused by the question, but shrugs it off and says, "Okay. I'll take you there. Driveway without a mailbox."

He keeps his word and brings the truck to a slow stop in front of the driveway. Upon noticing the pieces of the mailbox scattered across the bottom of the incline, he tries to look over my head and then around my head, hoping to get a view of the house at the end of the driveway. When he can't see it, he asks, "You alright, sir?"

"Just fine," I tell him. "Wait here. I'll be right back." I open the door and climb down, and then shut it.

"Where're you going?" I don't answer him and start limping up the driveway. "Hey! Where're you going?"

I enter the house through the gaping maw in the shutter door, and I strain against my broken toe as I clamber over the fallen shelf through the hole in the door into the pool room. I navigate through the house, noticing some areas in the ceiling have dampened; blood has pooled and seeped through, dripping to the floor in some areas. In other areas, streams of ash hiss quietly through small gaps made by the previous leakages of blood before the Maureens I killed up there also turned to ash when… well…

I walk into my room and retrieve my wallet off the night table, and I count the cash in it. Three hundred forty-five dollars.

I walk out the front door and limp down the driveway, nearly falling once or twice as I descend the incline, and I approach the truck. The driver's face is a picture of perfect curiosity. It lights up in confusion when I take all the money out of my wallet and hand it to him through the passenger window. "Here."

"Whoa, sir, I can't—I can't take that! It was just a ride, no big deal."

"Accept it," I tell him firmly. "I'm grateful for the ride." He still hesitates. "Take it!" I snap, making him jump.

"Y-you sure?"

"*Take* it, goddamn you!" He finally does, alarmed by my outburst.

I draw back, pulling my arm out of his window. I smile at him. "Thank you."

He nods gratefully and then pulls away, and I watch his truck grumble down the road until it disappears around the bend.

9:19 AM. Once again, I enter through the opening I made in the garage shutters. This time, I pick up the jerry can, which still has some gasoline in it. I take it back through the hole, up the ramp, and into the front door. I tip some gas on the rug and my wife's shoes and the kids' shoes and my shoes, and then I trickle some down the hall, and throw some on the bedroom floors, conserving it as I go, making sure the thin lines I pour out are all connecting. The bathroom, down the basement steps, through the kitchen, into the living room, then the dining area, and the pool section connected to it, out onto the deck, where I use up the last of it. I toss the jerry can away and look into the woods, expecting to see Maureen.

Of course, I don't.

I finish writing this journal, because now I know how it will end, and I gather the pages in a nice little stack and stuff them in an envelope, and in marker that I know won't bleed through, I write TO WHOM IT MAY CONCERN. Then I seal it, take it outside, and place it in the center of the driveway before returning inside.

The house feels so big and empty now. Still, I feel nothing, not even when I take a barbecue lighter from a kitchen drawer and a boning knife out of the block and set them on the coffee table. Then I go into the dining room and gather all the pictures Maureen had thrown onto the floor during her rampage, and I take them to the coffee table, too, and line them up in front of me.

Almost done.

I walk over the shelf and search the videotapes until I find one marked MEMORIES, and I replace *The Omega Man* with this one in the VCR and switch on the TV. I take a seat and I look at the display of old family photos I lined up. I look at every single one as a camcorder video starts on the TV. It's our wedding back in 1991, as recorded by my father. The priest Maureen and I are standing in front of finishes his passages, and he asks me if I'll take her as my wife. I never forgot how angelic, how breathtakingly beautiful she looked in her wedding dress. She literally *glowed*. I remember fighting back tears when I said, "I do." The priest of course asks her the same question about me, and her sweet voice replies, cracks a bit, as she's almost crying herself: "I do."

"You may now kiss the bride." Christ, do I. That first embrace in holy matrimony, now officially married, pressing our lips together, locking us in…

The picture changes to a year later, to my father carrying the camcorder into the hospital room catching Maureen and I with a newly born Todd in her arms. He looks so small and soft, delicately cocooned in Maureen's gentle embrace. My father says cheerfully, though quietly as to not wake our baby, "Who're my lucky lovebirds?"

Maureen giggles. I smile at the camera, at an older version of myself, before my father focuses the lens on little baby Todd. "There's my little nephew."

Now the tears return. I glance back down at the photos and select my favourite group photo of the five of us, Mary being only a year old when this was first taken. We're all standing in front of the house, *this* house, a proud couple with three beautiful children that had just bought their first house. Damn... that was a perfect day. We couldn't be happier then.

I pick up the lighter and set a corner alight and watch an orange circle of flame spread across it. I throw the photo onto the floor and it spins in half a circle before spiralling directly on the stream of gasoline. Flames zip down the line like cars in a circuit, into the kitchen, the living room, the hallway, down the basement stairs, in the bathroom, all three bedrooms. The flames spread faster on the bedroom carpets and the carpeted stairs, I'm sure. It's taking a while for it to spread anywhere on the hardwood floor, but soon enough, it does.

Next, the boning knife. I look at its blade, and then I slice it across my left forearm from my elbow to my wrist. The pain makes me jump, but it only hurts for a second, receding to a throbbing sting. The blood flows freely down my arm and drips on my leg and the couch. The knife trades hands. It hovers above my right arm, hesitant to feel the pain, no matter how brief, before I take a deep breath and repeat the same action. With both arms seeping, and the house beginning to burn around me, I have nothing else to do now, except lean back, and watch the memories recorded on this tape.

Michael's birth in 1994 has little three-year-old Todd all excited. "I'm gonna be a big brother! I'm gonna be a big brother!"

Maureen and I laugh at his enthusiasm. She's holding little baby Michael in her arms and says with a chuckle, "Todd. Todd, my love, you're *already* a big brother!"

Todd cheers, jumping hyperactively in his chair.

Fading. I'm fading. I can feel my energy slipping away. Not yet. Not yet.

Mary's birth, 1996. Both boys are standing on their own shoulder to shoulder, grinning up at the camera before their grandmother moves it away from them and focuses it on Maureen and I. For the final time, my wonderful wife is cradling a newborn baby in a hospital bed, and I'm sitting right beside her with an arm draped over her shoulder. Mary's sound asleep, nestled in her bosom.

"Congratulations, you two," my mother says. I can still see her smile on her weathered, gentle face in my memories when I was sitting on the other side of that lens.

She zooms in on us as Maureen leans slightly toward me and says to me, "I love you, Cameron."

I know this off by heart, of course, and the last thing I say, is in perfect sync with the younger me on the TV: "I love you more."

Maureen giggles again, and it's the last thing I hear. Her smile as she looks back down at our baby Mary is the last thing I ever see.

Ashes to ashes. Dust to dust.

Works by Alexander Engel-Hodgkinson

Clockworld (One-Shot)

The Tea Party Affair

I Keep My True Love in the Basement (One-Shot)

Reality Glitch ('Jumping for Charlotte' segment)

No Bounds ('Cranston & Layman' segment)

I Keep My True Love in the Basement/REMIX

Cobalt Christmas

She Watches Me Bury Her

The Final Apocalypse Saga (First two volumes previously published as 'Dark-Boy')

Cobalt Rogue, Vol. 1: The Dead Blue

Cobalt Rogue, Vol. 2: Sky Japan Welcome Party

www.ingramcontent.com/pod-product-compliance
Lightning Source LLC
Chambersburg PA
CBHW020640130626
46552CB00003B/1317